Unforgettable
Book 3

To Janayne

Happy Reading

MUAH

Nikki LiAnne

PRAISE FOR UNFORGETTABLE 3

"Wow! Nelle L'Amour has done a remarkable job with this series. I am definitely putting this one on my top reads for 2016."

—Brittany's Book Blog

"A totally epic love story! I've screamed, cried, and laughed out loud. Suspense, mystery, passion (loads by the way!), and plenty of drama. This series is definitely the best I've read."

—Jeanette Book Reviews

"Brandon and Zoey are definitely one of my favorite book couples. The minute this book hit my Kindle, I opened it and by the next day, I was reading the last line and thinking, 'Wow! That story was amazing!'"

—The Erotic Book Blog

"Wow! I was totally taken by surprise by the way things transpired and I LOVED it!"

—Wicked Babes Blog Review

"The conclusion to a magnificent series. This is a non-stop rollercoaster ride you cannot miss."

—As You Like It Reviews

"Action-packed, explosive, and well written. Nelle L'Amour is diabolically brilliant at writing twists and turns. Well placed humor had me laughing until my stomach hurt and the sexy scene goodness was SCORCHIN' HOT!"

—The Power of Three Readers

"Wow! I absolutely love this series. I may have my best series for 2016 already read in January."

—Alpha Book Club

"Wow, what an ending!! Nelle exceeded every expectation I had and more. Just read the Unforgettable series because you won't regret it!"

—Nerdy Bookworm

"What a great way to end the series. I loved this set of books. I found it extremely hard to put the book down."

—Kimmie Sue's Review

"The conclusion of Brandon and Zoey's story is every television show genre in one—there's drama...there's comedy...there's definitely steam, and the horror and reality factors play their part as well. When their story finally fades to black, readers will feel like they've been put through the wringer, which is exactly what I think Nelle L'Amour wanted us to feel!"

—The Fairest of All Book Reviews

Books by Nelle L'Amour

Unforgettable

BOOK THREE

NELLE L'AMOUR

To join my mailing list for new releases, sales, and giveaways, please sign up here:

NEWSLETTER: http://eepurl.com/N3AXb

NICHOLS CANYON PRESS

Los Angeles, CA USA

Unforgettable Book 3
By Nelle L'Amour

Cover by Arijana Karcic, Cover It! Designs
Proofreading by Mary Jo Toth
Formatting by BB eBooks

Dedication

To the late great Nat King Cole and his daughter, Natalie, whose unforgettable song inspired the story of Brandon and Zoey.

And to Jeanette Sinfield, my muse, who inspired me to keep going when I wanted to give up. Your love and support will always be unforgettable.

"Perfect moments can be had but not preserved, except in memory."

—Leonard Nimoy

Unforgettable
Book 3

Chapter 1

Brandon

The flicks of a warm, wet tongue graze my neck. The Gooch. I slowly peel open my eyes, one at a time. They feel like they've been super-glued together and the lids are made of cement. The pup wags his tail. I can't say the same for the one that's hung between my legs. It feels like a dead weight.

Squinting, I glance down at my watch. It's six a.m. The darkness of night has morphed into the light of day though the sky's a depressing gray. I must have nodded off. Still on the couch, draped in a thick towel, I feel sick to my stomach. And it hurts to think. Last night's events come at me like a rockslide. My head aches, my heart aches, and my cock aches.

Everything's gone wrong. My romantic getaway with Zoey here in Cannes has ended up a total nightmare. Fucking Katrina showed up and fucked up everything. I know she's crazy enough to follow through with her threat—to tell the media I physically assaulted her and threatened her life. My insane fiancée staged the whole thing right down to slashing her arm with a jagged piece of glass and pulling out clumps of hair from her head. But she's right. The media will believe her. She even took photos. Goddammit. She's blackmailing me. Holding a virtual knife to my chest to cut off my balls. Giving me no choice but to marry her and go along with her absurd wedding plans. I don't love her. I don't like her. I loathe her. There are bitches. Fucking bitches. And psycho bitches. She belongs in a category all of her own. Fucking psycho bitch.

Burying my head in my palms, I squeeze my burning eyes shut for a moment's reprieve. Hoping the blackness behind my lids will give me clarity to find a way out of this horrific mess. I breathe in and out of my nose as I search my chaotic mind. My thoughts are like bumper cars, colliding into each other, knocking any semblance of rationality off the track. It's futile. I can't think straight. Or think of a solution.

Zoey, Zoey, Zoey, Zoey. Her sweet name rings in my ears, silencing the cacophony. She's made for me. I love every ounce of her. Inside and out. The irony—it took amnesia to make me realize that the girl of my dreams was right there in front of me all along. Last night was the best, most powerful, and most sensuous one of my life. I couldn't get enough of her. She rocked my world.

Then goddamn Katrina showed up. The timing couldn't have been worse. A bitter cocktail of guilt and remorse courses through me. I shouldn't have let the fucking psycho bitch throw those demeaning insults at her. My beautiful Zoey kept her head up high and weathered the storm like the trooper she is. And I love her all the more for her courage, strength, and pride. My loyal little soldier. I'm the one who's the coward and should hang my head in shame.

Shit. I promised to text her, but I didn't. My poor Zoey. Knowing her, she must have stayed up all night waiting to hear from me. Confusion gives way to anguish. I owe her an explanation. It's all too convoluted to explain in an email. Let alone a text. An ugly conversation awaits me. I hope she'll understand. Maybe have a solution. Help me grow some balls and still love me for the powerless asshole I am.

I need to see her so fucking badly. I long to take her in my arms—smother her with kisses and love her as hard as I can. My fear of losing her holds me back. I sink my head deeper into my palms. The throb in my temples is nothing compared to the throb in my heart or the ache in my cock.

Finally, I will myself to face the inevitable with the remote hope of salvation.

Taking Gucci off my lap, I set him on the cushion next to me.

"Wish me good luck, Gooch," I mutter under my

breath. *Good luck for what?*

He barks.

"Shh!"

My legs unsteady, I rise from the couch.

"OW!" A sharp pain shoots up my leg. Holding onto the arm of the couch, I bend up my foot. Shit. It's bleeding. I've stepped on a small shard of glass, an unswept remnant of Katrina's insane rampage. A painful reminder I just don't need right now.

Keeping my heel up, I hobble to the closest bathroom with Gucci trailing behind me. Not the one Zoey and I shared last night that's adjacent to the master suite where Katrina's sleeping. The last thing I want to do is wake the bitch, though with her earplugs and sleeping mask, she'd probably sleep straight through a terrorist attack. I rinse my foot in the bidet, washing off the blood, while the memory of Zoey having an exquisite orgasm from the jets swirls around in my head. My limp dick twitches. I can't fight my need for her. The open wound is just another physical manifestation of my unwavering ache. My relentless desire.

I exchange the towel wrapped around my bare body for a fluffy bathrobe. I would have preferred putting on a fresh pair of sweats or some jeans, but my entire wardrobe is in the master bedroom as is my cell phone. Belting the robe, I head for the door to my suite. My injured foot hurts, but I can walk on it. My chest tightens with every painful step and my pulse accelerates. I don't know how I'm going to face Zoey without making her mine again. I want to chain her to me, then jump off the edge of the earth and hear her roar my name one last time… so loud the whole world will need hearing aids.

My pulse spikes while my cock sinks. Wishful thinking. In the bar area, I find a bowl that was spared in Katrina's wake of destruction and fill it up with water. I set it down on the floor, and Gucci immediately laps it up before cocking his head and gazing up at me with a "what's next" expression. With a firm hand command, I tell Gucci to stay and he obeys. I slink out of my suite and an envelope meets my feet.

One scripted word captures my attention.

~Brandon~

As elegant as the hand that wrote it. I'd recognize that handwriting anywhere. Zoey's.

Snapping up the envelope, I tear it open and read the contents. My eyes fly from the first line to the last.

Brandon~

This is goodbye. Thank you for giving me the opportunity to work with you. You can be sure I will honor our non-disclosure agreement and treasure our time spent together.

I will always remember you. You're unforgettable.

~Zoey ♥

My stomach clenches and so does my heart. Not wasting a second, I dash out of my suite as fast as I can and run down two flights of stairs to her hotel room. Breathless, I bang on the door.

"Open up, Zo."

No response.

I bang harder; I shout louder. "C'mon, Zoey. Open up!"

Bang! Bang! Bang!

An early morning housekeeper passes by me. Just in time before I knock down the door.

"*C'est ma chambre.* I've lost my key. Can you let me in?"

"*Mais, monsieur, il n'y a pas de personnes là.*"

"What do you mean?"

In broken English, the perplexed woman responds. "*La madame…*she check out."

What? She's gone? Panic grips me by the balls. I sprint to the elevator and pound the down button. The elevator doesn't come. I pound and I pound and I pound. Goddamn elevator. I'm about to dash down the emergency stairs again—all five steep flights—when a car finally arrives.

To my relief, it descends quickly to The Carlton lobby without a stop. As soon as the doors part, I dart to the front desk. Thank God, there's no line.

The attractive young clerk on duty is more than pleased to see me. She's the one who checked us in to the hotel.

"Ah! *Bonjour,* Monsieur Taylor. *Eez* everything okay?"

"*Oui.*" I nod. "Have you by chance seen my assistant?" I try to hide my panic.

"You mean, Mademoiselle Hart?"

"Yes, yes. I mean, *oui, oui!*"

The clerk smiles. *"Mais, oui.* She checked out an hour ago. She went back to *zee* States. *Pauvre petite!* Some kind of emergency."

"Get me a fucking cab right now!" *And pardon my English.*

The early morning rush hour traffic along the scenic N98 to Nice International Airport is impossible. Why does everyone and their mother have to be going there? It's like some kind of mass exodus from the South of France.

"Can't you go any faster?" I yell at the mustached cab driver.

"Je ne parle pas anglais."

Fuck. "*Plus rapido, s'il vous plait.*" My French sucks.

"*Pas possible.*"

Fuck again. I wish I had the Ducati. But after crashing it, the bike almost didn't make it back to the hotel last night. I should have taken a helicopter. At this point, by foot would be faster.

The traffic may be at a crawl, but my heart's beating a gazillion miles an hour. A toxic mixture of angst, frustration, and regret consumes me. I wish I had my cell phone so I could call her. The thought of borrowing the cabbie's phone crosses my mind, but I don't know Zoey's number since I have it on speed dial. I slump against the backseat lost in defeat.

Finally, we make it to the airport. What should have taken twenty minutes has taken over an hour. I slip the driver a hundred Euros and fly into the busy terminal. Jostling the crowd, still in my bathrobe and barefoot, I sprint up to the departures and arrivals board. There are two flights departing for Los Angeles in a few minutes—one, Air France; the other, American. Shit. Which one would Zoey be on? I opt for American for only one reason. Because it's how she prefers her Starbucks. Caffè Americano. Just like me. And because last night we shared a cocktail that also bore that name. I hope my hunch is right.

My heart in my throat, I bolt up to the American Airlines ticket counter, cutting in front of the long line. Assorted grumbles in French and English go in one ear and out the other. Yeah, I'm a fucking asshole in both languages.

The ticket agent is a very attractive brunette in her early thirties. The name on her badge is Jeanette. Her eyes widen at the sight of me.

"*Mon Dieu!* You're *zee* big Hollywood star. Brandon Taylor!"

"*Oui*. I need a big favor, Jeanette. Can you tell me if a passenger named Zoey Hart is on Flight 216 heading to LA?"

The agent bites down on her full red lips. "I am so sorry. I cannot do that. It *eez* against airport rules and regulations."

"Please! It's an emergency!"

"What kind of emergency?"

Think, Brandon, think...Got it! "She's my assistant and she's on meds. She left them behind. If she doesn't have them, she may create an incident on the plane. She's very bipolar. If she doesn't take her meds hourly, she gets extremely violent."

The attendant listens intently while my eyes glance at the clock. 7:45. Shit. The flight's departing in five minutes.

"Hmm. That *eez* very serious. I will call security."

"Hurry!"

Two long minutes later, a pair of security guards are flanking me. Jeanette tells them about the high-risk situation. I guessed right—Zoey's on the American flight.

"*Allons y!*" says one of them, instantly recognizing me.

Fame has its benefits. On my next rapid heartbeat,

I'm racing with them barefoot through the airport at lightning speed. My man-pack is flapping beneath my robe. I may have a heart attack. We barge through security and then zoom down a long, crowded corridor to the departure gate. Why does it have to be the last one?

Finally, we get there. Despite what good shape I'm in, I'm breathing heavily.

In French, the other security guard explains the issue to the airline attendant on duty. I listen with baited breath, my pulse pounding.

She shrugs. "*Ce n'est pas possible.*"

"What do you mean?"

"Monsieur Taylor, the plane has already departed."

"What!?" My heart crashes to the ground like a plummeting jet. "There's nothing you can do?" A thick layer of desperation and despair coats my voice.

"I am so sorry. We can send a message to *zee* flight attendants to keep a special eye on her. Perhaps, you would like us to book you on *zee* next flight. It departs at noon."

"*Non, merci,*" I rasp. I can't leave—the red carpet screening of the *Kurt Kussler* season finale is tonight. There's no way I can let Conquest Broadcasting and all the international broadcasters down.

Through the floor-to-ceiling windows, I watch the plane soar over the Mediterranean. As the plane ascends, my heart descends into a black hole, knowing I may never see my beloved Zoey Hart again.

Chapter 2

Zoey

It's all over the news. All over the Internet. The headline of every major tabloid.

Prince Brandon Searching for his Princess!

MIP: Missing Irresistible Princess: Where is She?

"There's Only One Princess for Me!"

Darkness at the Grand Palais. Prince Mourning Loss of his Dream Princess.

"I will find her!"—Prince Brandon

My heart aches so much it hurts to breathe. I cannot stop thinking about the magical time I had with him. Flesh to flesh, burning with desire. His magnificent royal cock inside me, taking me to the edge of the earth. And then the clock struck midnight. And the magic ended. I fled and turned back to the ordinary servant girl I am. He'll never find me. My evil stepsister Katrina and her equally wicked mother Enid keep me hidden. And now, they won't even let me leave the house. I'm their prisoner. Their slave.

Alone in my decrepit attic quarters, I cuddle Gucci, Katrina's adorable pup that she wants nothing to do with. The little white fur ball is my one solace in life. Well, along with one other—the life-size poster of The Prince that hangs by my bed. "Oh, Gooch," I lament, "Prince Brandon will never find me. According to all the news reports, he can't remember my name."

Gucci looks up at me with his big, brown puppy eyes. A tear falls from my watering eyes and dissolves into his soft fur coat. They keep pouring. I've shed so many tears since the ball I could fill an ocean. My precious Gucci gets up on his hind legs and laps them away with his warm tongue. I'm thankful for his sweet kisses. But I long for the kiss of another. The prince who'll never be mine.

"Zoella!" A manic voice cuts into my misery. Katrina. Now, what does she want?

"Get your fat ass down here immediately. The Prince will be here any minute, and I don't know what to wear!"

My heart almost stops. Prince Brandon is on his way? I leap to my feet and scurry to the cracked mirror standing in the corner of my room. I stare at myself. My hair is matted and my gaunt, puffy-eyed face is blotchy. My rags hang on my bones. In a word, I look terrible. I hastily smooth my hair and wipe away my tears, but nothing can disguise my pathetic state of being. An impatient Katrina shouts out my name again. With Gucci trailing behind me, I trudge downstairs.

My eyes grow wide. Katrina has all but emptied her walk-in closet. Glittery jewel-colored gowns are strewn everywhere—on couches, chairs, tables, and more. She tosses them about as if they're confetti.

"Oh, Mommy, I don't know what to wear. I hate being seen in the same thing twice!"

Nearby Enid surveys Katrina's choices. "Darling, what about the coral gown you wore to the ball. It was divine. And for sure, The Prince will recognize you in it."

Katrina scrunches her face. "I had it sent to the dry cleaner. Thanks to some fat whore, I took a tumble on the dance floor."

For the first time in ages, I inwardly smile at the memory of Prince Brandon shoving her out of the way. She shoots me a scathing look.

"Zoella, I need a new dress immediately! I want you to go to Barneys right this very minute!"

"B-but…" Oh no! If I go, I'll lose my chance to see The Prince. That's all I want…the chance to see His Gorgeousness once again. I desperately search for an excuse. "But the store doesn't open for another two hours."

"That's exactly the point. I want you to beat rush hour traffic and be there when the doors open. I'll arrange for my personal shopper to meet you. And besides, I don't want you around when The Prince arrives." She casts her venomous eyes down at Gucci. "Oh, and you can take that mangy mutt with you. The last thing I want is for him to bite Brandon."

Gucci growls at her. My heart sinks. Scooping up the little dog, I make a beeline for the front door. The roar of a motor and blasting horns stop me dead in my tracks. Spooked, Gucci jumps out of my arms and scoots away. A loud knock on the door follows.

"Open up!" bellows an unfamiliar voice. "His Royal Highness, Prince Brandon, requests an entrance."

My heart pounds in anticipation. Oh my goodness! The Prince is here!

Katrina screams in a panic. "Zoella, get your fat ass to the front door. But don't let The Prince in until I change into something appropriate. Stall him." Frenzy-eyed, she turns to her mother. "Mommy, help me!"

Enid scowls at me. "Zoella, what the hell are you waiting for? Go! Chop chop!" A double clap of her bony hands accompanies her last words.

My heart racing, I dash to the front door and open it slowly. My heart practically beats out of my chest. Standing before me on a rolled out red carpet is his Royal Gorgeousness dressed in his royal finery. A magnificent tux that's tailored to his inhumanly perfect body and complemented by his signature regal purple bowtie. On the street, an entourage of black limos is lined up behind his official car—a gleaming white Aston Martin convertible.

His violet eyes, two glistening jewels, meet mine. Neither of us can speak. Sparks fill my vision and my ears. I wonder if he can hear and see them too. That dazzling smile curls up the corners of his luscious lips, and he breaks the silence.

"Hi, do you live here?"

I clear my throat. *Brain to voice, come in please.* "I-I'm just a servant here. This house used to be my papa's, but now it belongs to my stepmother and her daughter."

He calls out to one of his entourage. "Niall, the shoe please."

At his command, a tall wiry man delivers the shoe on a purple velvet cushion. I inwardly gasp. It's the sparkling glass slipper I lost when I ran away from him at the palace.

"I am looking for the woman whose foot fits this shoe. If the shoe fits, something else will too. There's only one woman in the entire kingdom made for me."

Hot tingles all but consume me. Flushed, I glance down at my ratty sneaker-clad feet. To my astonishment, he tilts up my head by pressing his thumb under my chin. At his tender touch, I quiver with desire and lust.

His gaze holds me fiercely. "Are you going to let me in?"

In my head, I spread my legs wide and offer him the entrance to my pussy. I so long to have his royal cock inside me and to have his body on mine.

Before I can get my mouth to move, Katrina's sharp voice pierces my ears.

"Oh, Your Highness. I'm so glad you're here. You've come to the right place," she says breathily, joining us at the front door. She's dolled up in a bright yellow sequined gown that could light up the sky and a pair of matching stilettos. With her platinum hair cascading over her shoulders, the tall willowy blonde looks stunning. Frumpy me pales in comparison and a cloud of despair sweeps over me. I don't stand a chance with Prince Brandon.

She eyes the glass slipper. "Oh, Princey-Poo, did you bring that for me?"

"It belongs to the woman whose pussy fits my cock. I'm having every woman in Lalaland try it on. Whoever it fits will be my princess bride."

Katrina's feline green eyes light up. "What are we waiting for?" She shoots me a look that could kill. "Get lost, Zo-ey."

"Zoey?" The Prince repeats.

Before he can say another word, I do as I'm told. With a heavy heart, I retreat to my quarters. Little Gucci follows me.

I slump down on my rickety bed and bury my face in my hands. In no time, my palms are soaked from a deluge of tears. My chest heaves and my sobs sound in my ears. Beautiful Prince Brandon—the love of my life—will never be mine.

Only the sound of Gucci barking madly brings me out of my misery. I part my hands and glance down. There he is before me with the other glass slipper dangling from his mouth. It's one of his favorite toys. He drops it at my feet and then barks again at me. *Woof! Woof! Woof!* He's trying to communicate with me.

"What is it, little boy?" I sniffle.

Wagging his fuzzy tail, he picks up the shoe again in his mouth and runs toward the door to my chamber. With his front paw, he scratches at the slab of wood. I get it. He wants me to open it and follow him.

As I turn the knob, I hear Katrina screech. "Zo-eeeeee! Get your ugly face down here immediately. I need you!"

I wonder what my evil stepsister wants as I wind down the stairs with Gucci trailing closely behind me.

"It's about time you got here," she snaps as I set foot in the living room.

"Push harder!" screams her mother, rolling her eyes.

"I can't!" grunts Katrina.

I have to bite down on my bottom lip to contain my laughter. Katrina is trying to squeeze her size nine foot into my size six shoe. No matter how much she tries, she can't. With each squeeze and grunt, she turns redder than the crimson sole of her Louboutin.

"Zoella, use your hands, for God's sake, to stretch out the shoe," she yells.

"Katrina, it's not going to stretch. It's made of glass."

"Glass, my ass. Just do it!"

"Chop chop!" snaps a frustrated Enid.

Having no choice, I oblige. Taking the shoe into my hand, I tug at it. Of course, it doesn't budge. I need a glassblower. Prince Brandon's gaze stays on my hands—the same hands that once locked with his and circled his majestic shaft.

"Zoey, your hands are exquisite. Almost magical," he says.

"Thank you," I reply softly and then silently thank my beloved late Mama from whom I inherited my long, slender fingers.

The Prince's glimmering eyes remain on me. "Zoey, why don't *you* try on the slipper?"

"What!" shrieks Katrina before I can say a word. "There's no way that peasant's skanky foot belongs in that shoe. It's fit for a Beverly Hills princess like me!"

Brandon ignores her and, to my astonishment, bends down to untie my grungy sneaker. He tugs it off my right foot and flings it. My eyes stay on him as he caresses my sensitive sole, rubbing a spot in the center that sends a rush of tingles straight to my pussy. There must be a string attached. Then, he reverently kisses the instep. His warm lips on my flesh make me melt. It takes all I have to keep my balance. My bones liquid, I'm falling apart.

"Zoey, your feet are as beautiful as your hands. So soft and tender." He takes the glass slipper from me before it falls out of my trembling hand. I'm close to swooning.

"Zoey, hold on to me while I slip on the shoe."

I grasp his powerful bicep as he gingerly slides the sparkling slipper onto my foot. My foot is halfway in it when suddenly a hand snatches the shoe away. Katrina!

"Say goodbye to your future!" she sneers, and on my next breath, she hurls the delicate slipper to the hardwood floor. *Smash!*

"No!" I cry out. Tears fill my eyes as I watch it splinter into smithereens, the spiky six-inch heel detaching from the sole.

Katrina smiles smugly. "Brandon, you're wasting your time with this slovenly peon. I'm the one for you. Let's just get the hell out of here and ride your Aston Martin into the sunset. Mommy will start planning the wedding. *I'll* be your Cinderella bride."

She clutches a stunned Brandon's arm and yanks him away from me.

"Wait!" With a sharp jerk that sends my evil step-sister flying, he breaks away from her. "Look!"

Craning my neck, I follow his gaze. Oh my God!

It's Gucci, carrying the other slipper in his mouth. He scampers up to us, and before the little dog deposits the shoe, Prince Brandon seizes and beholds it.

"It's the other slipper!" His eyes, lit with excitement, burn into mine. "I have at last found my princess bride. I just knew it the minute I set my eyes on you. It's you, Zoey! The woman I've dreamt about and searched high and low for."

"What!" screams a shocked Katrina as he effortlessly slips the stiletto onto my left foot. It fits perfectly. On my next rapid heartbeat, he scoops me up in his strong arms and his lips come crashing down on mine. My tongue finds his, and entwined, they waltz just like they once did at the ball. A sweeping, sensuous dance of love fills the walls of my mouth. Cupping his gorgeous dface, I squeeze my eyes shut as I fall deeper into his passionate embrace. I'm seeing stars.

"Mommy, do something!" Katrina whines like a bratty two-year old, but there's nothing either she or her mother can do. My Prince has come, and I'm never going to lose him. He's mine. And I'm his. Our mouths stay locked as he carries me out the door.

"Ow, you fucking beast!" I hear Katrina cry out.

Peeking with one eye, I glance her way. HA! Gucci has bitten her, giving the bitch what she deserves. Proudly wagging his tail, the little dog follows us outside. He belongs to The Prince and me now.

When we reach The Prince's stately car, he finally

breaks the kiss and dismisses his entourage. Opening both eyes, I watch the fleet of black limos drive away.

"Are you taking me back to your palace?" I ask between little kisses on his face and neck. He tastes so delicious.

He sets me down on the hood, close to the edge. "Zoey, I can't wait that long. I'm taking you right here. Right now." Removing the glass slipper and throwing it into the regal convertible, he simultaneously yanks off my sweats and little lace panties. My sweatshirt and bra are next. He tosses everything to the pavement. I'm totally bared to him in broad daylight. His lust-filled eyes roam down my curvaceous body inch by inch.

"Oh, my sweet Princess, you're so exquisite. Even more beautiful than I remember." He gropes my heavy breasts and lifts them to his mouth. His mouth clamps down on my nipples and he sucks them. I'm so aroused a puddle must be pooling on the Aston.

A hand reaches for my pussy, and he caresses it. A soft moan escapes my lips.

"Oh, my beautiful, sexy princess, it feels just like I remember it. So silky and wet." He finds my clit and rubs it with his thumb. My head arches back in pure ecstasy.

"Don't stop!" I plead.

"Hold on, baby." With glazed eyes, I watch as he undoes his pants. His enormous cock springs out as they slide down his long muscular legs. I can't help but reach for it, wrapping my fingers around the base. It feels like hot pulsing velvet.

"Oh, baby, that feels so fucking good. The perfect fit. Only you. Spread your legs and put it where it belongs."

He leans into me as I part my thighs at his command and put his mighty crown to my entrance. I'm so soaking wet that he shoves the entirety with all its glory into me on a single thrust, taking me to the hilt. I cry out from the tinge of exquisite pain and then scream with divine pleasure as he begins to fuck me royally. I wrap my legs around his hips as he slides me closer.

"Oh, my Lord! My master! Fuck me hard!" I grip his broad shoulders so as not to slip off the car and rock my hips to meet his powerful thrusts. I clench my muscles around his relentless rigid length as he claims me.

"There's only one way with you, my beautiful princess. You're mine now. Totally mine. Yes, I'm your Lord. Your master. I'm going to fuck you for eternity. Love you until forever. And give you the happily ever after you've always wanted and truly deserved. But tell me, I'm yours."

"Oh my gorgeous Lord, I'm yours for forever. I've never stopped loving you. And will never. Even in death, you will live in my heart. You have my undying love."

"Jesus, my little princess. You're making me crazy

with your sweet surrender. I'm going to give you an orgasm you'll never forget. Everyone in the kingdom will hear you cry out my name. But I want you to come with me. Can you do that?"

"Yes," I pant out, unsure if I can, as much as I want to please him and have that incredible experience of oneness. Waves of ecstasy sweep through my body as I gauge his own climax. He's close, so very close because I can feel his searing length pulsate inside me.

Then, suddenly, he stops pummeling me and after a deep, feral grunt, he roars out my name. It's more like a wail—the cry of a wild animal that's been mortally wounded. I don't think he's come. I would have felt the explosion and his release. He collapses upon me, his dead weight almost knocking me over. I snap open my eyes and gasp. Hovering over us is Katrina. A wicked, triumphant smile snakes across her face.

"Say goodbye to your Prince Charming!" she snickers.

"What have you done?" A sudden wave of panic washes over me, and then reality stabs me so hard I feel my heart bleed.

"Oh my God! Oh my God!!" My six-inch glass heel is wedged deep in Brandon's back. An inordinate amount of blood soaks through the fine fabric of his jacket. I watch in horror as she slowly withdraws the sharp, bloodied spike. I immediately put my hand to Brandon's wound, hoping I can stop the flow of his blood. It's futile. The warm crimson liquid seeps through my fingers, but I can feel his labored breaths. The small rise and fall of his chest. Oh my God. He's still alive but barely.

"Oh, my Prince. My Lord. My Master! Please don't die on me! Please!!! His cock grows limp inside me. All life is ebbing from him. Sobs wrack my body. With my free hand, I fist his silky hair and lift up his head from my breasts. His eyes are open just a sliver, allowing a glint of violet light to slip through the lids. He sees me, and the faintest of smiles curls his lush lips.

"I swore, I would kill for you...and die for you, my sweet princess. Only for you." His voice is a mere whisper.

"No, No, No! Oh Brandon, my love! Take that back! Don't leave me! Please don't leave me! You promised you'd love me forever!"

"I...will...love...you..." Each word is a harsh breath. "For—"

Impulsively, as he takes his last breath, I slam my lips onto his, and parting them, I breathe into his mouth. Aren't kisses in fairy tales magical? The kisses of life?

In my ears, Katrina's maniacal laugh reverberates. "You pathetic girl. Fairy tales don't come true. Such stupid urban myths. There's only an eye for an eye; a tooth for a tooth. You took him away from me. And now, I've taken him away from you." She laughs again, more maniacally and louder.

"You wicked bitch!" I sob out. The sequins of her dress blind me.

"You know what they say. Nice girls finish last. Time to say goodbye to your life, you fat slut!"

"NOOOOOOO!!!!" A deafening scream pours out of my mouth as she aims the sharp heel dripping with blood between my eyes. Gucci barks madly, but it's too late…

Fade to black. In a cold sweat, I blink my eyes open and try to take hold of my bearings. I'm dazed and confused. And sobbing.

"Are you okay, Ms. Hart?" comes an unfamiliar female voice before I can get a grip. How does she know my name?

Reality slaps me across the face at the realization of my real-life unhappily ever after. Still blubbering, I nod. I'm on a plane, heading back to LA. I must have fallen asleep and had a terrifying nightmare. Katrina took Brandon away from me. Destroyed my fairy tale dream. My waking life, however, is far more devastating. Brandon succumbed to her. He chose her over me. And he let me go. I'm bereft of both the job and the man I loved with all my heart and soul. Beautiful memories of Cannes do a slow, sad dance in my head until they're abruptly curtailed by the email Brandon sent me. With my eidetic memory, I can see the cold-hearted words in my mind as if I'm reading them off a computer screen. *I have no choice but to terminate your employment contract effective immediately.* He even threatened me with legal action should I ever talk to the media about him. I hit delete, but the bone-crushing words are permanently etched on my brain. I wish I could forget them. And forget him. Delete him from my mind. Rip him out of my heart. My soreness prevents me. I can still feel the sting of his lashes on my ass and the throb of my pussy with the hum of the plane. My clit aches as much as an open wound. I know these sensations will go away, but the ache in my heart will always stay. Brandon Taylor will always be unforgettable. My shoulders heave and my wails grow louder.

"Are you sure you're okay?" asks the flight attendant again, her eyes narrowing with concern. "Are you having some kind of episode?"

The word "episode" only upsets me further. I was supposed to be going to the red carpet screening of the last episode of *Kurt Kussler,* the season finale, with Brandon tonight. But now, he'll be going with another. America's stunning It Girl—his fiancée, Katrina. How could I have been so blind? So blind, so naïve, so stupid? I gave myself to him—my body, my heart, and my soul. And now all that remains is a pathetic skeleton of who I am. There's nothing left in my life that matters. I fight back the nausea that rises to my empty chest and manage two little words: "I'm fine." I'm so very far from fine it's a joke. I choke back sobs against the giant lump in my throat.

The flight to Los Angeles is estimated at ten long, painful hours. My sobs lessen, but the tears continue to pour. The flight attendants pay special attention to me. There's always a set of suspicious eyes on me as if I may be some kind of threat. I don't eat a thing, but when I ask an attendant for some wine, she refuses to serve me any, saying it may not be good for me in my condition. Soon afterward, another attendant sweeps down the aisle and gives me the evil eye. When I go the bathroom, one of them follows me and waits outside the door. I swear everyone's acting like I'm bipolar or some kind of terrorist. I'm not. Can't they tell I'm simply heartbroken? I've lost both my job and the man I love. I let myself be used. I fell for an act. Seeking an escape, I put on my headset and choose Celine Dion's "Love Theme" from *Titanic*. No, my heart won't go on. The tears multiply until I can cry no more. I close my eyes and let her beautiful voice lull me back to sleep.

Upon landing in Los Angeles, two flight attendants insist on accompanying me to baggage, and after I collect my one bag, an airport official helps me hail a cab. It's pouring rain—something rare for LA. The gloomy weather is fitting. Sheltering me with an umbrella, the young Latino lands one quickly.

"Where to?" asks the craggy driver.

I give him Brandon's address so I can pick up my car and my possessions. Though emotionally and physically drained, I'd better do it now with neither Brandon nor Katrina there. Due to the heavy rain and a few accidents along the way, it takes almost two hours to get to the Hollywood Hills. Numbness sets in during the long ride. And my cell phone dies. We finally reach Brandon's private street. My chest tightens; my pulse quickens. The cab winds up the long, twisting road; flooded, it's practically a river. I soak it in, knowing I'll never drive up it again. As we pass the spot where Brandon had his accident, a pang of sadness stabs me and a dark cloud shrouds my heart.

When we arrive at Brandon's gated property, I lower my window and reach out my hand to punch in the security code to let us in. The massive iron gate slides open. The driver pulls into the long driveway and stops in front of Brandon's front door.

"Nice place you have here," he says.

"Thanks," I mumble, handing him my credit card. I take care of the exorbitant hundred-dollar fare, tipping him generously. Grateful, he kindly helps me carry my bag to the front door and then due to the rain, he runs back to his car and takes off. The cruel droplets pelt me as I run through the private entrance to the guesthouse. As the sky continues to cry, my eyes cry too.

Once inside, I don't bother packing. All of Brandon's furnishings are staying so all I need to take are my personal belongings. Soaking wet and teary-eyed, I hastily gather them up and throw everything into my

Mini, making several trips. There's only one thing remaining—my shattered *Kurt Kussler* poster. Chilled to the bone, I stare at it, and as my teeth chatter, the tears fall faster.

"I hate you, Brandon Taylor. Do you hear me? I hate you!" Marching up to the poster, I give it a hard, angry kick. To my astonishment, it resists further damage. It's as if Kurt Kussler is invincible. Mocking me. *I can hurt you, but you can't hurt me. Get it. Got it? Good.*

Fuck it! Fuck him! The large poster, which won't even fit in my tiny overstuffed car, is staying behind. It'll be a house warming present for the bastard's next unfortunate assistant.

Burning with rage, I peel out of the driveway. Ironically, I arrived at Brandon's house in the pouring rain and now I'm leaving it in the pouring rain. As a rare lightning bolt flashes in the dark gray sky, that first fateful day flashes in my mind. The live wire of electricity that connected us when our fingertips touched is as vivid now as it was then. I fell for him hard and fast. I didn't even think I could work for him without falling apart. In retrospect, I shouldn't have. A painful knot of regret balls in my stomach. My aching heart clenches. Rage gives way to sorrow. The rain falls harder. My tears fall harder. Drenching me. I turn on my windshield wipers. If only I had a pair to swipe at my fast and furious tears. The electronic gate slides open and I tear through it, not looking back in my rear view mirror. As I whip down the hill, an afterthought about the poster hits me. Not about collecting it. But rather leaving it outside his gate for garbage collection. Too late. There's no going back. My life with Brandon Taylor is over.

Between the rain and my tears, it takes all I have to concentrate on driving. The roads are slippery and flooded. For LA, a heavy rainfall is like a blizzard. Praying I won't get into an accident, I drive straight to Pops and Auntie Jo's, taking La Cienega rather than the freeway because I'm in no shape for speeding, lane-changing idiots. Bleary-eyed and shivering, I drive slowly. The thunderstorm mirrors the torrent of emotions raging inside me.

I make it there safely. Thank God, Auntie Jo's home. One look at my tear-soaked face, she knows something's wrong. She also knows I wasn't supposed to be back from Cannes until the end of the week. At the front door, she gives me a hug. In her warm, comforting arms, my sopping wet body heaves sobs, the tears falling as fast and hard as the pellets of rain.

Chapter 3

Brandon

Thank God for my acting skills. It takes all I have to walk down the red carpet and flash a big smile at the hordes of paparazzi and spectators trying to get a shot of me. My heart is in my stomach. All I can think about is Zoey. She's been on my mind all day. I counted down the minutes till she touched down in LA. I know from checking with American she landed safely at 10 a.m. West Coast time, but she hasn't responded to my numerous phone calls, emails, and texts. I even tried her every which way before I left the hotel. And still no answer. I so badly need to talk to her, though I'm not quite sure what to say. Maybe I can, at least, woo her back to her job. Offer her double the salary and all kinds of perks. Who am I kidding? She won't come back. Truthfully, I don't think she'll ever speak to me again. I fucked up. If only I hadn't dozed off. I should have told her what went down with Katrina right away, but she fled before I had the chance. Now, I'm not sure if I'll ever have the chance. As if it really matters. I can't have Zoey. I've been trapped by the psychopath into a loveless marriage that I don't know how to get out of. Believe me, Katrina made it loud and clear before we got here that she would expose her gash and tell the media I assaulted her if I made one wrong move—right on the red carpet before thousands of spectators if she had to. She's got me by the balls. Every nerve's on edge.

"Bratrina! Bratrina!" the crowd roars wildly. I wish they'd all shut up. Katrina, on the other hand, decked out in a sleek silver sheath, hangs like a piece of jewelry from my arm and is relishing every minute of the hoopla. Wearing long matching opera gloves that cover her bandaged arm, she waves to the crowd and blows kisses. Flashing her dazzling smile, my sicko fiancée gives the paparazzi everything they could hope for. The walk down the red carpet feels like an eternity. Along the way, a chill sweeps over me. While the weather in Cannes has been perfect up until now, the air is now brisk and damp. April showers are in the forecast and they could start tonight.

Click! Click! Click! Click! Everywhere I look the flashes of cameras blind me. I'm sure photos of us will be plastered all over the Internet way before the screening ends. In fact, they could be up in mere minutes. A dark thought besieges me at the entrance to the theater. Shit. What if Zoey sees them? For sure, she'll think Katrina and I are back together again and in love. My stomach bubbles with sudden panic. Though she must loathe me, that's the last thing I want her to think. I've got to reach her before the photos go viral! But with the screening and Q&A session, that's going to be next to impossible. I'm fucked every which way I turn.

While movies at the prestigious Cannes Film Festival usually screen at the stadium-sized Grand Théâtre Lumière, Conquest has set up a more intimate screening for five hundred broadcasters from around the world at a much smaller but elegant Art Deco theater in the center of town. The theater is jam-packed. A stunning blond usher, who could be a starlet herself, escorts us to the front row.

I take a seat next to Blake Burns and his wife Jennifer. They're both wide-eyed with shock to see me with Katrina, who remains standing.

"Why, hello, Blake, darling!" breathes out Katrina, bending to give him a double cheek kiss. Visibly repulsed, Blake doesn't stand up or return the favor.

"Where's Zoey?" he asks me after Katrina and Jen exchange icy hellos.

Katrina shoots me a look that could kill. My skin heats under her scathing gaze. "Um, uh, she had to go back to LA. An emergency came up."

Concern washes over Jen's face. "Oh, Brandon, I'm so sorry to hear that. I hope everything's all right."

Nothing's all right. I have the burning urge to blurt out everything, but Katrina's a dangerous ticking time bomb. With a haughty fling of her platinum mane, she responds to Blake's wife before I can.

"Jennifer, everything's *perfectly* fine. Nothing to worry about."

Smirking, she sits down next to me and clasps my hand for good measure. Her gloved fingers feel like fetters holding me prisoner. The rest of the *Kurt Kussler* cast, along with the series' show runners, take their seats, sparing me from having to talk more about Zoey's whereabouts. Perceiving her only as my assistant, they have no idea I planned on taking her to the red carpet premier of the *Kurt Kussler* season finale. Everyone's here—my co-stars Kellie Fox, Jewel Starr, and Jibran Abdoo (the big-hearted French actor who plays my nefarious nemesis, The Locust) as well as Executive Producer Doug DeMille and Jewel's husband, Director Niall Davies. Also sitting in the front row are Blake's parents, who flew in earlier today—Saul Bernstein, the venerable head of Conquest Broadcasting, and his elegant wife, Helen.

The theater filled, Blake runs up to the stage amidst thundering applause. He welcomes everyone and then, without further ado, tells the eager audience, "Relax and enjoy the exciting season finale of *Kurt Kussler.*"

As he returns to his seat, the lights dim and the red velvet curtain rises. Butterflies swarm my stomach. This is the first time I'll be viewing the completed episode with sound effects and music.

The crowd enthusiastically applauds again when the opening credits roll on the big screen. "Get it! Got it? Good!" they shout out in unison with my gun-wielding character at the end. Goosebumps. Wow! I seriously didn't know they were *that* into *Kurt Kussler*. I wonder if that's what home viewers do each week when they tune into the show.

Following my signature line, *Kurt Kussler: Season 5 Finale Screener* pops up on the screen followed by: *Written by Brandon Taylor.* At the sight of my name, the audience yet again breaks into raucous applause, complete with cheers and whistles. I'm at once humbled and blown away. Excited and nervous. My skin prickles. For the first time in my career, I've been credited as a writer. This episode was my idea. My dream. My reality. One small thing's missing—a title. I still haven't thought of one, and the ones that were bounced around in the writers' room didn't do it for me.

Another onslaught of butterflies assaults my stomach as the special two-hour episode begins. Will they like it? Playing without commercials, it'll run approximately ninety minutes. The theater is so quiet you can hear a pin drop. I swivel my head to check out the audience; even in the pitch-black theater, I can tell they're spellbound. I return my attention to the screen, and I'm spellbound myself. The episode looks amazing. Our editing team has done such a great job, and the state-of-the-art sound system and big screen make it even more compelling to watch.

Close to the conclusion, Katrina, who I've all but forgotten about, whispers in my ear. "Darling, I have to use the restroom."

"Fine," I whisper back. "And don't bother coming back," I add silently.

Letting go of my hand, she rises and exits. I'm glad to be rid of her. My eyes stay riveted on the big screen, and my stomach muscles clench. The romantic tension between Kurt and his assistant Mel is heating up. Something that's always been there, and now at last, it's coming to a climax. I wrote this scene so quickly it was as if the words were flying out of my brain. Or perhaps my heart. Emotionally, it's hitting me so hard I'm not sure I can watch it. My chest tightens painfully. And then, *BANG!* It's over! Loud gasps fill the theater along with audible sniffles and sobs from female audience members. The screen fades to black. The lights go back on while uproarious applause and chants of bravo bellow in my ears. I turn my head. Holy shit! A standing ovation! I'm overwhelmed. It's almost as big a moment as winning the Golden Globe.

Blake gives me a man hug. "Brandon, they fucking loved it! Congratulations, man!"

My fellow cast members and the production team also congratulate me with exuberant embraces. I give a special hug to my co-star, Kellie Fox, whose extraordinary portrayal of Kurt's impassioned assistant Mel contributed so much to the impact of this episode.

"It's Kellie's night as much as mine," I humbly tell everyone.

"Oh, Brandon, the finale was wonderful! Totally heart-wrenching!" Blake's teary-eyed wife Jen gushes before smacking my face with a kiss. "It's really a shame Zoey couldn't be here."

Her words hit me like a punch to my gut. *My Zoey.* Yes, she should have been here. That was my intention—to have my adorable assistant experience the episode with me. To show her what she means to me. My eyes flit to the vacant seat next to mine. Katrina's still MIA, but I don't give a damn. I'm glad she missed the gripping, emotionally charged climax. That scene belongs only to Zoey. She may be six thousand miles away, but deep in my soul, I'm sharing this triumphant moment with her. Maybe Katrina could steal her seat, but she can't rob me of the place Zoey has in my heart. She's the love of my life, even if I can't have her anymore. My high gives way to the depths of despair. My heart aching, I call on my acting skills again to plaster a big smile on my face as I head up to the stage with Blake and the rest of the cast and crew for a short Q&A session. Chairs have been brought out for our comfort.

Questions from the audience are tossed our way at a rapid fire pace. While some are directed at my co-stars and Executive Producer Doug DeMille, the majority of them are targeted to me. Several ushers with mikes in their hands dash around the audience to handle the queries. So many have their hands raised, eager to ask one. For sure, given our twenty-minute time frame, we won't be able to get to all of them. A cocktail reception in the lobby awaits us and perhaps those who are not chosen can interact with us there. Personally, I just want to get the fuck out of here. I'm in no mood to schmooze. Wearing my tux, I play with my father's lucky gold cufflinks and think of Zoey as the questions come hurling at me.

Q: "Brandon, what was it like writing your first episode?"

Me: "It was very challenging. But I was very inspired."

Q: "What inspired you?"

Me: "The question should be: Who inspired me?"

Q: "Okay, who inspired you?"

Me: "Someone I love."

Q: Your fiancée, Katrina Moore?"

My heart stammers and then I answer:

Me: "No."

On my next agonizing breath, Katrina re-enters the theater and saunters back to her seat. All eyes are on the platinum-haired beauty. I avoid eye contact with her and am thankful the usher moves on to someone else before I have to answer the question—"Who?"

Q: "Can we expect to see the relationship between Kurt and Mel to flourish next season?"

I hesitate.

Me: "I'm not sure…"

My voice trails off. My dark reality consumes me. Our relationship, if you can call it that, is already over. Zoey and I will never be. Words are trapped in my throat. Blake, to my relief, chimes in.

Blake: "We'll be focus-group testing the episode right after it airs to make sure we're going in the right direction. But previous groups, with both men and women, loved the idea of Kurt hooking up with his assistant Mel."

Mumbles of approval sound in the theater.

Blake: "We have time for just one more question."

An attractive, petite Asian woman is selected among the many who are zealously waving their hands and crying out: "Me, me, me, me!" Animated, she gives her best shot at English.

Q: "*Bwandon*, I want to ask you a *pawsonal* question. You excited about upcoming *mowage* to *Katwina, Amewica* It *Gawl?*"

Her question catches me off guard. Before I can say a word, Katrina leaps up from her seat and turns to face her. "Of course, he is. It's going to be the wedding of the century. And please, if any of you would like to attend, just let me know. Mommy will send you an invitation. We'd love to have you. It's going to be televised live—a special edition of my reality series. I'm sure you'll all want to air the episode on your networks as well. It's going to be a ratings block-buster!"

Mortification races through my bloodstream. Jesus. She's already invited half the world to our wedding. And now the whole world may get a chance to watch it. My body wants to jump out of my skin, leap off the stage, and shout out, "Fuck you, Katrina!" End it right here, right now. Put the kibosh on Bratrina and follow my heart. But I know if I did that, all hell would break loose. The fucking psycho bitch would tell the world I assaulted her. Fling off her glove and the bandage beneath it to expose the damage *I* did. Then, show everyone the photos on her phone to prove it. God knows what else she would say or do. It would create a media frenzy. Without a doubt, kill the ratings of *Kurt Kussler* and destroy my career. *"Brandon Taylor: It Girl Slayer."* Would Blake Burns, who knows she's evil and demented, come to my rescue? The question really is: Could he? It doesn't take a lot of soul-searching to figure out the answer. It's simply no. The raving lunatic is out of control. Totally uncontrollable. Chances are anything Blake would say or do would come spitting back in his face. Possibly even destroy *his* career and marriage. That I'm caught between a rock and a hard place is the understatement of the century. Even if I once really loved Katrina and I doubt it, that can never be possible again after what she's done. I will never forgive her nor will I feel for her what I feel for Zoey. I've always loved Zoey. But sadly, she will soon just be a memory in the vortex of my mind. Blake once shared his father's words of wisdom with me. Some things are meant to be forgotten. Not Zoey. A sickening feeling sweeps over me. Amnesia comes with its benefits.

Katrina's pompous voice hurtles me back to the moment. "Does anyone else have a question for *me*?"

Is she fucking serious? To my relief, an incensed Blake ends the Q&A session and shuts her up. I still don't know exactly what went down between the two of them. He's been tight-lipped about it. Even over drinks on the plane over here, he wouldn't spill the beans. Maybe I can get further with his wife Jennifer. But what's the point? That's not going to make the nightmare go away either.

Heading out the side door, I retreat with Blake and the others, who participated in the Q&A session, to the lobby where the cocktail reception is underway. I need a drink desperately. Before I can get to the bar, broadcasters from all over the globe swarm me. It's like a shark feeding frenzy—the whole world wants a taste of me. Either to have their picture taken with TV's number one action star or have me autograph the official *Kurt Kussler* photo they received in their swag bags. I'm every man's macho aspiration and every woman's fucking fantasy. Out of the corner of my eye, I catch sight of Katrina flitting about, posing with one broadcaster after another for the paparazzi and Conquest publicity photographers.

It doesn't take long before I'm feeling claustrophobic. Tightness of breath and dizziness are accompanied by beads of sweat that break out across my skin. Blake Burns comes to my rescue and pulls me aside.

"You okay, Brandon?"

"Yeah," I lie. "Just jet lagged."

"You did great with the Q&A."

"Thanks."

"I'm curious. Who was your inspiration?"

"Zoey." I blurt out her name.

"That's what I thought. Why did she end up going back to LA?"

"It's complicated." My fallback word.

He harkens back to our conversation on the plane. "Are you still having second thoughts about marrying Katrina?"

My jaw tightens. "No." I change the subject when I see her making a beeline our way, champagne in hand. "Listen, Blake, would you mind if I cut out early? I could really use a good night's sleep."

"Sure. No problem. I'll have security get you out

the back way." He wraps an arm around me. "Pal-y, sometime later this week after the convention, let's meet for a drink at The Carlton bar, okay?"

I agree to his request. Five minutes later, I'm in a dark alley outside the theater. Balls. It's raining. Pouring. Coming down like a spray of bullets. In a matter of seconds, the violent pellets soak me. Chill me to the bone. Shivering, I dip my hand into my pants pocket and pull out my cell phone. With the nine-hour time difference, it's early afternoon in always-sunny Los Angeles.

I speed dial Zoey. Once again, her phone goes straight to voice mail.

"Hi, it's Zoey. Leave a message and I'll call you back."

Her sultry rasp guts me. Leaving no message, I try again. Nothing. I text her: *Call me as soon as u get this message.*

Gripping my phone, I continue to walk. The needles of rain sting me as I await a response. Nada. Growing frantic, I call her one more time. Again no answer. After several more attempts, I finally leave a message. "Zoey, I need to talk to you. Please. Call me!" I only hope my desperate plea isn't drowned out by the pounding rain. With only a glimmer of hope, I wait for a call back and then my phone dies. My heart hits rock bottom. There's no doubt in my mind she's seen photos of Katrina and me hand-in-hand on the red carpet. Last night, I was fucking her. Loving every minute. Loving all of her. Tonight, I'm totally fucked. And I hate who I am. Showing no mercy, the relentless rain hammers me as I turn onto the Croisette. A cruising taxi, hoping for a passenger, pulls along the curb, but I wave it away and let the pitiless rain bombard me. Totally soaked and painfully numb, I trudge back to The Carlton, knowing I may never see or hear from her again.

Chapter 4

Brandon

I don't know how I make it through five long, tortuous days at MIP. My only saving grace is I rarely see Katrina during the day. She spends most of her time shopping with Gucci along the Rue D'Antibes while I hang out with Blake and meet with broadcasters and licensors from around the world at the swamped Conquest Broadcasting booth inside The Grand Palais. My nights, however, are an entirely different story. She's wrapped around me like a noose and insists on going to every dinner and event I'm invited to. We're the darlings of both the press and paparazzi. They can't get enough of Bratrina. Photos of us together are splattered all over newspapers in Cannes and I'm sure all over the world. Not wanting to make myself sicker than I am, I've totally avoided the Internet. I'm sure it's a Bratrina fest.

Finally, on the last day of the conference, I have a chance to sit down with Blake for a drink at The Carlton Bar. He's managed to score us a corner booth that gives us a modicum of privacy in the bustling Belle Époque space. It's a popular spot among broadcasters to hang loose after a busy day at the convention. I'm dressed casually in ripped jeans and a T-shirt while he's in a sleek, dark suit that's tailor made for his body. Blake may look like an actor, but first and foremost he's a businessman. And let me tell you, after seeing him in action on the floor, he's great at his game.

Over expensive Scotches, we start off with small talk about MIP.

"We rocked it," says Blake after a gulp of his cocktail. "Thanks to the screening, we renewed the show in every major territory at a premium price and even picked up new broadcasters along with lucrative licensing and merchandising deals."

Since I have profit participation, that's going to be a big chunk of money to me. Yet, right now, I could give a shit. "That's great," I say, my voice lackluster.

"Brandon, you don't seem too excited."

I take a swig of the Scotch. "I am. I'm just tired and stressed."

"Brandon, I'm going to level with you. I didn't ask you to have drinks with me to talk business. I'm worried about you, bro. You're our biggest star. And a friend. I need to know what's going on."

I shift in the booth and take a deep breath. "It's Katrina. I have a problem."

His brows knitted, Blake takes another sip of his drink. "Problem isn't the right word. Katrina's a fucking nightmare. I've tried to tell you this."

I take another chug of my Scotch and set the tumbler down. If Blake's going to open up to me about their past, it's now or never. Here goes. "What went down between the two of you?"

Blake drains his Scotch. He breathes in and out through his nose. "Listen, man, this is what I can tell you. She almost cost me my life and my marriage."

"Jesus. She tried to kill you?"

"Not quite, but she could have. She's a fucking psychopath."

His words sink in. Did she run me over and leave me for dead? Did she intend to kill me last night in her rampage?

Blake continues, cutting my disquieting thoughts short. His eyes flicker with rage.

"And when we were in high school, she did something really sicko that hurt both me and my family."

Questions are burning on my tongue, but I can tell Blake's being cryptic. He's not going to tell me everything, at least not tonight. He plays with his empty tumbler while I try to extract more information.

"After my lunch with you back in January, she told me you were the love of her life and you broke her heart."

Blake huffs and shakes his head in dismay. "She's so fucking delusional. I was *never* in love with her. She couldn't handle it and had a breakdown. She was sent to a mental institution after we graduated."

Christ. She really is insane. What have I gotten myself into? I polish off the Scotch. Blake orders another round from a passing waiter.

"So, what shit is she doing to you?" he asks me while we await our drinks.

"She's blackmailing me."

Blake furrows his brows. "What exactly do you mean?"

Loosened up by the alcohol, the words tumble out. "If I don't marry her, she's going to tell the media I assaulted her and tried to kill her."

Blake's crisp blue eyes widen. "Did you?"

"Christ, no! She staged the whole thing in my hotel suite and then took photos with her phone to prove it. She has a self-inflicted gash on her arm that must be six-inches long. She's been covering it up."

"Jesus."

"I know. It's a fucking nightmare."

Just in time, the drinks arrive. We're both in dire need of them and take several gulps.

"I fucked up, Blake. And I hurt someone else really badly."

"Your assistant, Zoey?"

My lips press thin. "Yeah. I'm in love with her. Katrina caught us together. That's what set her off. I intended to break up with her before this trip, but the timing was off. She went out of town to visit her father in prison and wasn't reachable."

"It's water under the bridge at this point. Trust me, the psycho bitch would have figured out a way to bring you down."

Despite Blake's comment, I bow my head with guilt and remorse. "I should have never brought Zoey here."

"Don't be so hard on yourself. You did what any guy would do."

"Yeah, I listened to my cock."

"No, you listened to your heart."

I look up, lifting a brow as Blake continues.

"While going after my wife Jennifer—and that's a wild story for another time—I did some seriously stupid things but learned my cock is connected to my heart."

I digest Blake's words. He must be right. At the thought of Zoey, the ache in my heart gives way to an ache in my cock. I still haven't been able to reach her. It's like she's shut me out of her life.

"Does Zoey know what's going on?"

"No. She split from Cannes right after Katrina showed up. I'm positive she thinks I went back to Katrina because she wrote me a goodbye forever note." The moving words of that letter make my heart stutter and I pause. "I haven't been able to reach her."

We both imbibe our drinks in silence, our faces pinched in deep thought.

"Blake, I don't know what to do."

Setting his tumbler down, Blake blows out a breath of hot air. "This is really fucked. I don't know either. If she goes to the press, all hell will break loose. And even if I came to your defense, it's going to be an ugly shooting match—your word against hers. The public adores her. Her clout-score is through the roof. And the timing couldn't be worse with the season finale of *Kurt Kussler* airing only two days after your highly anticipated televised wedding. Ditch her and you may kill the show. And your career."

Pending doom. Swelling with despair, I sweep my hand across my forehead and then along my jaw. "I know. Fuck. Blake, I'm sorry."

"Don't be sorry. It's not your fault."

Blake cheers me up a bit in what is otherwise a dire, futile situation.

"If you don't mind, I'm going to talk to my wise old man. He's a whiz when it comes to shit like this."

"Thanks, but I'd rather you not." The thought of Saul Bernstein, the mighty head of Conquest Broadcasting, knowing my fucked-up dilemma is unsettling to say the least. Blake's father's words of wisdom, which he shared during our lunch on the lot, whirl around in my head. "Sometimes it's better to forget than remember."

If only I could make everything with Katrina disappear with a snap of my fingers…abracadabra. It's not going to happen. Out of the corner of my eye, I see the psycho bitch strutting our way—Gucci in one arm, a dozen designer shopping bags dangling from the other. A long-sleeved cashmere cardigan camouflages her bandaged wound.

"Well, well, if it isn't my two favorite men doing some male bonding," she coos as she approaches our booth.

"Hello, Kat," Blake says icily.

"I hope you and Jennifer will be coming to our wedding."

Blake narrows his eyes at her. "Not if we can help it."

A suspicious Katrina shoots me a scathing look. "Don't fuck with me, Brandon, if you know what's good for you." And then she turns to Blake. "*We'll* expect you both there." She turns on her heel and saunters away.

Blake and I exchange a look of doom. Then, he orders another round of drinks.

Chapter 5

Brandon

Back from Cannes after five tortuous days, I let the driver bring my bags into my house while I dash to the guesthouse. A ray of optimism brightens my forlorn state. The lights are on. I knock loudly on the front door.

"Zoey, are you there?"

No answer.

I bang harder. So hard I shred my knuckles.

"Zoey, if you're there, open up!"

Still no answer.

"Dammit, Zoey. I know you're there. Stop playing games with me."

Adrenaline pumping through my veins, I'm ready to knock down the door but on a whim try the doorknob first, giving it a jiggle. To my surprise, the door swings open and my eyes grow wide. The place looks like it's been ransacked. My first thought, a dark one, almost suffocates me—oh no, Donatelli got to her! While the bastard who murdered both Zoey's mother and my parents was the last person on my mind in Cannes with all I had to contend with, he now totally consumes me. My heart pounds so forcefully it hurts to breathe. Then my heartbeat calms down when I realize all her personal belongings are gone. Empty closets and cabinets have been left wide open as have drawers. A few are strewn on the floor. There's only one thing that remains in her bedroom—a shattered *Kurt Kussler* poster. The one I gave her for Christmas and didn't even bother signing. My heart leaden, I gather it into my hands and transport it to my house. I feel like I'm carrying some dead version of myself. Reality sinks in—Zoey's gone for good. She said goodbye in her note and she meant it. There's someone I need to call.

Setting the poster against a wall in my living room, I scavenge my house. Where the hell did I put it—her father, Pete's number? He handed me a business card the first time I met him; it's got to be here somewhere. After a desperate search in which I turn the house upside down, I finally find it tucked under my computer in my office. Pulling out my cell phone from my jeans pocket, I immediately call his number. He picks up on the first ring.

"Detective Pete Billings, LAPD."

"Hi, Detective, it's Brandon…Brandon Taylor."

"Hello, Brandon." The coldness in his voice could freeze over Lake Michigan in the summer. It unnerves me.

"Um, uh, sir, I've been trying to reach Zoey. I-I'm worried she lost her phone."

A beat of silence. "No, Brandon, she didn't lose her phone."

"Is she all right?" Panic creeps into my voice.

"No, as a matter of fact, she's not all right."

Fuck. Does he know what happened in Cannes? Chances are he does. Zoey's very close and open with her father. She's the apple of his eye.

"Is she ill?"

"Yes, Brandon, she's very ill."

My heart thuds in my ear. "What's wrong with her?"

"You know as well as I do." His voice rises with anger. *He knows.*

A long beat of silence on my end. Guilt and remorse claw their way up to my vocal chords until I have to clear my throat just to be sure I can talk.

"Can I possibly see her?" I sound like a frightened mouse.

"No, Brandon."

"Can I possibly talk to her?"

"No, Brandon."

"Detective—"

He cuts me off, but the truth is I don't know what to

say. Words are failing me.

"Listen, Brandon, I want you to stay out of Zoey's life. You've hurt her enough. I, for one, cannot bear to see my little girl hurt any more."

"I didn't mean to." My voice is so small I can barely hear myself.

"Brandon, I don't need or have time for your bullshit. And please don't call me here again."

"What about my hit and run case?"

"There's been little progress. We still can't trace Donatelli, and there are no new leads that link him to your manager Scott."

"I learned some interesting things about Katrina while I was in Cannes," I say, hoping this will warm him up to me.

"For obvious reasons, my colleague, Lieutenant Mancuso, will be handling your side of the case. I will pass this information on to him, and I'm sure he'll be in touch. In the future, please address all your inquiries to him and anything you may discover that might be of importance. Goodbye, Brandon."

Click. The line goes quiet. He's hung up on me. Tossing my phone onto my desk, I trudge back to the living room and pour myself a Scotch before slumping onto the couch. Facing the shattered poster, I drain the tumbler in a single gulp. The alcohol burns straight through me, pouring deep into the hole in my chest. I stare at the shattered poster; it's as broken as I am.

Jetlag mixes with the alcohol, creating a lethal cocktail of fatigue and despair. Katrina, who went on to Milan, will be back tomorrow and the nightmare will persevere. Just get worse. For a minute while I was on the phone with Pete, I thought about telling him that Katrina was blackmailing me. But reason got the better of me—if he knew what I did sexually to Zoey, he might think I'm some kind of sick pervert who gets off on hurting women. And, of course, once back in LA, the psycho bitch would defend herself and run to the press with her "evidence."

I'm fucked. Zoey's gone. Unattainable. I reach into the breast pocket of my leather jacket and pull out my one souvenir of what we had in Cannes. I managed to salvage them before Katrina flushed them down the toilet. Zoey's scanty black lace panties. They're still alive with her scent, my scent, the sea, and the sky. I put them to my nose and inhale them. Their intoxicating smell makes me drunk with desire and regret.

Zoey, Zoey, Zoey. I wish you were mine.

Chapter 6

Zoey

"Love is a disease for which there is no cure." Mel once said that to a distraught Kurt in an episode of Brandon's series, and now I know it's true. Since coming back to LA, I haven't left my bed. It's been five long, sickening days. Every bone, every muscle, every cell is infected with him.

Trapped in a fluish haze, I drift in and out of sleep, and if it weren't for Auntie Jo looking in on me and bringing me some homemade soup, the only thing I can manage to get down my throat and just barely, I wouldn't know if it were morning, noon, or night. When I'm conscious, all I do is cry and think about him. I used to have fantasies, but now my mind is filled with painful memories. All the good times we had together play in my head. I can't shut them down. Even when I drift off into a fitful sleep, he's in my dreams.

Kissing and fucking me. Holding me in his strong arms. Dancing and loving me. The melody of Mama's favorite song, "Unforgettable," links all the beautiful memories together like a never-ending music video. Oh, why can't I forget? Amnesia would be God's gift.

"Do you want to talk about it, honey?" Auntie Jo asks, the next time she treads lightly into my room with a tray in hand.

"Please, Auntie. I can't. Not yet." My voice is a hoarse whisper I don't recognize. Forcing myself to sit up, I take the bowl of soup from her and take a few sips to satisfy her that I'm eating and won't die. She has no clue my heart's been broken by Brandon Taylor. All she knows is that I've lost my job and contracted some flu from the rain. Pops knows the truth, and he's promised me he won't tell her until I do first. I may never.

Pops is as concerned about me as much as Jo is. For the fifth time this week, he stops by my room after coming home from work. The lights are off and I'm under the covers. I have no clue what time it is.

He sits down beside me on the edge of the bed. "Babycakes, it's been almost a week. You've got to face reality again."

"Pops, I can't. He hurt me so much."

"He called me today at the precinct."

My heart jumps. I bolt to a sitting position. He's back!

"He wants to talk to you. He says he's been trying to reach you."

I've had my cell phone turned off with his number blocked and have vowed to get a brand new number so he can never reach me. A frantic thought claws at me.

"Pops, did you tell him where I am?" My throat's so raw it hurts to talk.

"No."

I should sigh with relief, but I'm aching to see him. I just can't. What would be the point? To torture myself? My heart's endured enough pain to last a lifetime.

"Thanks, Pops," I croak, verging on more tears. "Please don't ever tell him my whereabouts. I never want to see him again. Never!"

The last words come out with a choked sob. Pops takes me in his brawny arms and lets me cry for as long as I need to. At least fifteen minutes pass, maybe more. It's so hard to tell time in this dysfunctional, heartbroken state.

He smooths my damp, ratty hair that hasn't been combed in days. Auntie Jo barges in. She must have heard my sobbing. Worry is etched on her face.

"Pete—"

Pops gently cuts her off. "She's okay."

She joins Pops on the bed, brushing my forehead, out of love and concern. She probably thinks I have a fever. I do, but it's raging in my heart.

"Honey," she says softly, "it's just a job. I know you liked it, but there are so many you can get. You're so smart and efficient. Who wouldn't want to hire you? I bet you can even land another good position with a big star."

Unable to talk, I nod my head weakly and sniffle. There's only one star in the sky for me. But it's fallen and lost its shine, leaving a burning hole in my heart.

Pops cups his hands on my quivering shoulders and looks deep into my watering eyes. "Babycakes, it's time to tell Jo the truth about what's going on."

I swallow hard past the golf ball-sized lump in my throat, and finally, tearfully, I open up. "Auntie, I fell in love with Brandon Taylor. I did something I should have never done with him."

"Oh, dear Lord!" She clasps a hand to her mouth. "You—"

I nod with a mixture of remorse and embarrassment.

"Sweetie, forget that I'm your mother and tell me everything!"

I just love Auntie Jo. Underneath that sweet demeanor, there's a wild woman with a heart of gold. I tell her about our romantic evening, beginning with our beautiful candlelit dinner and continuing with our sensuous swim in the Mediterranean, leaving out explicit details about Brandon's sexual prowess and proclivities, as she quietly hangs on to every word, her eyes wide and unblinking. I can't tell what's going through her head. It's probably hard for her to believe that her plain Jane daughter had an affair with her idol. *People Magazine's* "Sexiest Man Alive." And the truth is it's still surreal for me. Grateful that she asks me no questions, I flick my eyes to Pops for encouragement to go on. He nods and I continue.

"After the swim, we went back to his hotel suite…and then his horrible fiancée, Katrina, showed up."

"Oh no!" gasps Auntie Jo.

"And to make a long story short, while I was waiting in my room for him to come back for me, he sent me an email and fired me."

Just as I'm about to burst into more tears, Jo takes me in her loving arms and hugs me.

"Oh, you poor dear. I know exactly what you're going through."

"You do?" I stammer, expecting her to reprimand me for my foolishness.

"Yes. I had my heart broken too. And by a man I worked with—the owner of my beauty shop. I was secretly crazy about him. I worshipped him. Dreamt about him every minute of every day. And then he hired an assistant who was the most beautiful girl I'd ever seen. He was totally smitten by her, and within a month, they were engaged. I cried for days and even stayed home from work."

I'm all ears. I never knew this. "What happened?"

"I had to leave my job. The pain was too great. I couldn't face seeing him every day, knowing the man of my dreams could never be mine."

"How did you get through it?" My voice is a little stronger.

Pops chimes in. "Yours truly."

Auntie smiles and clasps his hand. "It's true. I thought I could never love another man, but I healed. Then, Pete came into my life. Stepped into the new salon where I was working for a haircut and swept me off my feet. I've never looked back."

Pops beams. "And she better not. It was the worst haircut I ever got because she was so smitten by Mr. Handsome here."

Auntie Jo chuckles and gives him a peck on the cheek. "If you want to know my opinion, it was the *best* haircut I ever gave."

Their sweet, loving exchange warms me, taking me out of my deep funk. Pops holds me in his intense gaze, the gaze of a detective who doesn't beat around the bush. "You know, Babycakes, finding the right person is like digging for a clue to solve a crime. True love…it's out there somewhere. You just gotta keep looking."

Auntie chimes in. "There are a million people you can love and who will love you. It's just a matter of finding one. Just one is all it takes."

I thought I'd found him. But he didn't love me

back. I take a long, deep breath. Air fills me like helium. It's time to pick up the pieces and start over again.

My stomach growls. "Auntie, what's for dinner?"

Chapter 7

Zoey

My heart will go on. Shattered pieces still beat. Over the next few weeks, I learn that there's a truth to the *Titanic* love theme lyrics. While every night in my dreams I still see him, I recover from my heartbreak enough to resume a normal everyday existence. The heart is a mighty organ. Even broken, it can still pump life into you. Each day I grow stronger, and by the end of the month, I've found a place of my own to live—a small but charming one-bedroom apartment in Beachwood Canyon. Plus a new job—a masseuse at Posh, a high-end spa on Sunset. The timing was perfect. One of their therapists had just gone on maternity leave, and with my credentials, I was a shoe-in for the position. While I feel like I've regressed a little, I tell myself it's only temporary until I figure out what I really want to do.

My new job is not fulfilling, but it helps pay the rent and keeps me from dipping into my savings. Though I only work in the afternoons and have weekends off, I don't enjoy being holed up in a small massage room and physically exerting myself. Been there, done that. I didn't like it the first time around. And I like it even less now. The clients, mostly super rich, are demanding and often ungrateful.

Once upon a time, I had a dream to become an actress. I enrolled in a few acting workshops after high school but abandoned them, discouraged that a full-figured girl like me couldn't succeed. And hence, I went to an occupational school and became a certified masseuse. But working for Brandon and helping him with his lines gave me another taste of the craft. A yen. The more I despise my new job, the more the acting bug gnaws at me. I apply to several local acting schools—mentioning my former experience (I throw in the fact that I played Adelaide in my junior high production of *Guys and Dolls* to make my resumé look longer) and the fact I was the personal assistant to a major Hollywood star (I'm not allowed to disclose Brandon's name because of our confidentially agreement), and include a headshot. Rejection after rejection. Disheartened, I'm about to give up when I get an invitation to audition for one of Hollywood's most prestigious institutions. The Bella Stadler Academy of Acting!

My audition is on a Saturday. I wake up bright and early, shower, and dress. I choose simple jeans, sneakers, and a short sleeve crew-neck tee. My online research told me to dress conservatively and to *not* wear a skirt (my first choice) to avoid the possibility of pulling a Sharon Stone in *Basic Instinct*. Nope, that wouldn't look too good, especially with my thighs. With the monologue I've chosen in a manila folder, I head over to the Academy which is located off Holly-wood Boulevard, a mere ten minutes from my house. I have the lines memorized, but go over them in my head during the drive. My heart gallops with both anticipa-tion and apprehension. *Lead your dreams and land them.* I so want to be accepted.

What I didn't count on was the lack of parking spots and the congested traffic due to construction on every corner. The Bella Stadler Academy of Acting doesn't come with valet parking. Every nearby meter is taken. Crap. The last thing I want is to be late for my audition. Anxiety pulses through me. Finally, after circling the school three times in stop and go traffic, I eye a van pulling out of a spot a few blocks away. I whip into it and fly out of my Mini, running to my destination so I won't miss my audition. Somewhere between Yucca and Las Palmas, a rather shady area populated by drug dealers and addicts, I realize I've left my monologue in the car. Shit. I'll have to live without it. There's no time to go back for it.

The Bella Stadler Academy of Acting is a narrow, non-descript two-story red brick building sandwiched between a Greek yogurt joint and a deli in the middle of Las Palmas. You'd never know it was a prestigious acting school except by the name of the school on the marquis and the fact that there's a long line of hopefuls that look my age lined up outside, all studying their monologues. Breathlessly, I survey them and a ball of intimidation curls in my gut. Everyone looks so Hollywood beautiful and stylish. Of course, no guy comes close to Brandon, but the girls are all tall, bronzed, wafer thin want-to-be starlets with lustrous manes that look like they belong in a L'Oréal commercial. Katrinas. My skin bristles at the thought of her. Maybe I should have dressed up more and worn something different. Going back home, however, is not an option.

"Um, uh, excuse me," I ask a stunning Emma Stone lookalike, who has her nose buried in her audition piece. "What do I do?"

Shooting me a dirty look for breaking her concentration, she tells me I need to go inside and sign in at the reception desk. And then get in line. Her voice is as cold as dry ice. She immediately returns her attention to her audition piece. I check in and then head to the end of the line. I breathe in the intensely competitive air.

Finally, after almost two hours of waiting in the rising heat, it's my turn. Butterflies flutter in my stomach and my heart's racing. *You can do this, Zoey!* I've practiced my monologue a gazillion times, both aloud and in my head. I've got it down pat. The receptionist, a jovial effeminate man, tells me to head down the long corridor to Audition Room 3. My heart thumping, I take anxious steps until I'm there. I turn the doorknob, feeling like I'm about to jump out of a plane. Oh, please God, don't let me forget to pull the chord of my parachute. I've got to make it through this and score a landing.

The high-ceiling audition room is a mini-theater, with a small stage and several rows of vintage, ruby-red velvet theater chairs facing it. A shocking, familiar throaty voice greets me as I take in my surroundings.

"Well, Miss Hart, I certainly hope you can do a lot better than the dilettantes I've seen thus far," she huffs, scanning my pathetic resumé.

Oh my God! It's legendary Bella Stadler herself! Brandon's mentor! The beautiful woman I met at the Joshua Tree spa. She turns her head and my gaze meets hers. She's seated in her wheelchair in an aisle at the end of the front row. Her crinkly, gray eyes sparkle at the sight of me. Instant recognition.

"How lovely to see you again, my dear."

"The same," I stutter, so in awe of her. She's clad in a bohemian, ankle-length lavender dress with a paisley shawl that complements her smooth olive skin, deep-set eyes, and loose, waist-long silver hair. Despite the tremors, she looks healthier and more stunning than I remember. The Ayurvedic spa treatments must be working.

"So, my dear, did it work out with your gentleman friend?"

My breath hitches in my throat as a wave of sadness washes over me.

"Unfortunately, it didn't," I reply, not letting her know that it was Brandon, one of her most illustrious students. I don't want anything to jeopardize my chances of getting into her academy. Nor do I want to embark on a conversation about my personal life and my former boss. I banish him to the back of my mind.

"I'm sorry to hear that." Her husky voice is warm and genuine. "But these experiences are put into our lives to enrich it and draw from."

"Yes, I agree." My voice is shaky.

"Let me ask you, why do you want to become an actress?"

"It's always been a big dream of mine. I pursued it and gave up. I'm finally ready to lead my dream and land it." I paraphrase the wise words Bella shared with me at the spa with conviction and passion.

Smiling warmly, she folds her shaky hands in her lap. "Let's get down to business then. What have you chosen to perform?"

"Juliet's last soliloquy from *Romeo and Juliet.*"

Her smile widens. "Excellent. Please begin."

"Where would you like me to perform it?"

"On the stage, of course."

I stumble onto the stage. Drawing in a deep breath, I launch right into it. After a little bit of a rough start because I'm jittery with nerves, the words flow. Getting down on my knees, I transform into Juliet, the tragic maiden who falls in love with a devastating man she can't have who has taken his life to be united in death with her. In my mind's eye, I see my Romeo—Brandon—before me, his beautiful face permanently etched in my brain.

"O happy dagger

This is thy sheath

There rust and let me die."

In true method actor fashion, I channel all my emotions and memories of him into my words. Tears spill from my eyes as I plunge an imaginary dagger into my heart. *Oh the pain!* I collapse onto the stage floor, so emotionally drained from my performance that I can't lift myself up. Three faint claps sound in my ears.

"Bravo!"

I slowly raise my head and, with tears streaming down my cheeks, face Bella. She's glowing.

"That was absolutely brilliant! The highlight of my otherwise mundane day and, by far, one of the best auditions I've ever witnessed."

I'm waltzing on a cloud, in a state of disbelief. "Really?" I ask, my voice a mere squeak.

"Yes, my dear. Only one other student blew me away like that." A wistful smile spreads on her lips. "And he went on to win a Golden Globe."

Brandon. She must be referring to him. My chest tightens. "Does that mean I've been accepted to your program?"

"My dear, please show up next Saturday morning for your first class. Horatio at the front desk will give you the course list and syllabus on your way out. And if you need any financial aid, please let him know. We're well-endowed thanks to our generous alumni."

I'm still speechless and on my knees when Horatio enters the theater and wheels Bella away. A rollercoaster of emotions sweeps through me. Shock. Excitement. Happiness. I've been accepted to the Bella Stadler Academy of Acting! By Bella herself! And then suddenly, I realize I'm probably crouched on the very spot Brandon stood upon many times before. Perhaps he even lay right here playing Romeo. A powerful, painful connection to him rips through me as a sob pushes into my throat. There's still a knife in my heart that I can't pull out.

Chapter 8

Zoey

I live for my acting classes. I attend three mornings a week and all day on Saturdays. Ranging from "On Camera Scene Study" to "Intensive Shakespeare," they get my mind off Brandon, though I would be lying not to say they keep me connected to him in some sick way. Though I've never seen her again, Bella is some kind of medium that keeps his spirit alive as much as I want to bury it.

The classes also help me stop dwelling on my mother's killer—Frank Donatelli. To my frustration, Pops's investigation has been moving forward at a snail's pace; the elusive Donatelli is nowhere to be found and clues to his whereabouts don't abound. Though Brandon's hit and run may be connected to Donatelli, I refrain from asking my father about the status of that investigation. All I know is that his colleague, Lieutenant Mancuso, is handling it.

It doesn't take long for me to realize I've discovered a passion. The acting workshops are intense, but I love them. They give me the chance to completely transform myself into another person and not hold back. I'm able to act out my emotions and be a master of my actions and words. While memorizing lines can be challenging, with my eidetic memory, it's a piece of cake, much to the envy of my classmates. Both my peers and instructors think I have real talent. I'm humbled. Many want to know if I've had previous experience. I tell them I took a few acting classes after high school, but wasn't serious. I don't, however, tell a soul that I was Brandon Taylor's personal assistant. No one needs to know.

Nor do I tell anyone about my birthday. On Monday, May eleventh, exactly one month to the day that I fled from Brandon and Cannes, I turn twenty-five. I have no big plans. I'm just having dinner with Auntie Jo and Pops. Auntie has promised to make me my favorite meal—her delicious roast beef with mashed potatoes and Yorkshire pudding. It's been a while since I've had a real meal. Between work and my acting classes, I've been surviving on take-out and ramen noodles. You'd think I'd stuff myself to fill the emptiness I still feel so often, but it's just the opposite. Heartache has decreased my appetite. If there's one thing for which I can be beholden to Brandon, I'm the thinnest I've ever been in my adult life. I'm a size eight. Okay, a plus size by Hollywood standards but a dream size for me.

After a stimulating acting class in the morning and my last massage client in the early evening, I head over to Pops and Jo's house in Culver City. With the ridiculous rush hour traffic, it's almost an hour drive. I flip on the radio and my heart fists.

"Unforgettable"—the Nat and Natalie version—is playing. A torrent of emotions hits me as tears trickle down my cheeks. I think of Mama. I think of him. To make matters even worse, I pass a gigantic billboard promoting the season finale of *Kurt Kussler* with a three dimensional Brandon aiming his gun. On the other side of the street is one of Katrina, practically naked and clutching Gucci, promoting her live televised wedding to Brandon at the end of the month. I'm so emotionally distraught I run a red light and narrowly miss being hit by another car. An angry horn blasts in my ears as I pull over to catch my breath. Trembling and teary-eyed, I turn off the radio. But I can't turn off my emotions. I can't fucking forget him. I can hardly breathe.

Despite my unstable condition, I manage to make it to my parents' house. After parking on the street, I ring the doorbell. The front door swings open and a loud "Surprise! Happy Birthday!" resounds in my ears. My jaw crashes to the floor. Oh my God! Jeffrey and Chaz are here too! I thought they both were away on business—Jeffrey in San Francisco for a billionaire's son's bar mitzvah and his fashion designer fiancé Chaz in D.C. for a trunk show, but they've both flown in for my birthday. And to top things off, my event-planner brother has decked out the house with Mylar balloons and a glittery disco ball for my silver birthday. Stevie Wonder's "Happy Birthday" blasts on the stereo system as I run up to give them each a big hug. The frown I was wearing earlier is replaced by a smile. I love them both. They've been so instrumental in my healing process. They loathe Brandon as much as I do, calling him every pejorative name in the book of gay insults, from douchebag to bitch.

I'm simply wowed. The dining room table is spectacular, draped with shimmering silver fabric upon which exotic white flowers in tall silver vases and silver candleholders are artfully arranged. We all take a seat. Just Pops is missing.

"Where's Pops?" I ask Jo, looking her way with admiration. God bless her. After telling her about the Brandon affair, she swore off *Kurt Kussler,* which was a huge, selfless sacrifice, considering how much she loved the series, especially this season's episodes. So looking forward to the season finale, she even donated her signed DVD collection and photo to Out of the Closet, a local charitable thrift store. The bottom line: she wants nothing to do with the man who broke my heart.

Before she can respond to my question, I hear a car

pull into the driveway.

Jo smiles. "That must be him now."

Two minutes later, Pops, still wearing his ubiqui-tous trench coat, joins us. He's carrying a huge flat carton. It must measure four feet by six.

"What's that?" I ask him as he sets it down against a wall.

He plunks down in the vacant chair at the head of the table. "It's something for you. It came to my office today."

I knit my brows. "Who's it from?"

Draping his coat on the back of the chair, he shrugs his shoulders. "No idea. There's no return address."

"Open it! Open it!" singsongs Jeffrey who loves surprises.

"Maybe it's from a secret admirer," chimes in Chaz.

I let out a little laugh. "I don't think so." There is one guy in my acting classes who seems to like me, but he has no clue today's my birthday. Nor does he know where Pops works.

"C'mon, Zoester, open it!" urges my impatient brother.

"Okay, okay." With my sharp meat knife in hand, I amble over to the huge package and slice through the center seam with the blade's serrated edge. The hissing sound of the splitting cardboard gives me goosebumps. With the long slit I've made in the box, I'm able to peek inside. My eyes grow wide and my breath hitches in my throat. I'm totally taken aback.

Oh my God! It's the *Kurt Kussler* poster I left behind at Brandon's place. Except now it's in a brand new frame with glass and it's signed.

♥

Brandon Taylor

My emotions teeter between rage and anguish, the latter winning by a landslide. Bile rises in my throat.

The fucking, fucking egotistical bastard. How could he do this? Torture me, make me suffer on my birthday? Though it was on my resumé, he never acknowledged it before. In fact, he made me work straight through it. The fucker. The sadistic fucker. How dare he put himself in my face? My lungs constricting, I blink back traitorous tears.

Jo's sweet voice intercepts my emotional turmoil. "Honey, what is it?"

Her query can read two ways. What's inside the box? Or what's going on inside me? I opt for the former interpretation.

"Um…it's just a poster I ordered from Crate & Barrel for my new apartment," I stutter. "I-I had it sent to Pops's office just in case I wasn't home."

"Ooh! I want to see it," croons Jeffrey.

"Yeah. C'mon, show and tell," coos Chaz.

I meet Pops's discerning gaze. His keen mind can

cut through bullshit like a knife. He knows I'm lying up my ass.

"Um, uh, I'd like to keep it in the box. I don't want it to get messed up in my car."

Jeffrey and Chaz shout "Boo" in unison. Jo unknowingly comes to the rescue.

"C'mon boys, behave. Leave Zoey alone. You'll see it when she hangs it up in her new apartment. And by the way, you must see it. It's really quite charming."

I quirk a fake smile. Inside, I'm falling apart into a million little pieces.

As I stumble back to my seat, Jo excuses herself to serve dinner.

Nausea washes over me. My appetite gone, I pick at my food. And when Auntie Jo brings the extravagant homemade buttercream cake to the table after the main course, I barely have the strength to blow out the twenty-five sparkling candles plus the one for good luck. The loudly sung words of "Happy Birthday" drift into my ears.

The day Mama died was the unhappiest birthday of my life. Despite thoughtful presents from my family, including a month's worth of acting lessons from Pops and Auntie Jo to supplement my scholarship and a gorgeous ivory spaghetti-strap dress from fashion designer Chaz, this is a close second.

My heart splintering, I make a wish. Despite the good luck candle, I know it won't come true.

Chapter 9

Brandon

Why won't she call me? Or text or email me? It's been over a week. I know she must have gotten the poster. I called the precinct and Alma at the front desk told me that Pete was in the office when a messenger delivered it. A noble, thoughtful gesture. I even added a heart above my signature. In retrospect, maybe I fucked up. I should have written, I love you, but I was hoping she'd call and I could say those words to her on the phone. Scrunching her little panties in my hand and nursing a Scotch in the other, I sink deeper into despair. Slumped on the couch, I stare at my cell phone on my lap. I'm losing hope. Stupid fucking me.

I've been an utter basket case since Cannes. With *Kurt Kussler* on hiatus until July, I haven't even had work to distract myself. While I should use the time to start on the outline of next season's premier episode, I can't get motivated. For all intents and purposes, Kurt Kussler is dead and I'm barely alive.

The last few weeks have been pure hell. If I could, I'd drink myself to oblivion, spend my days in bed, the covers over my head, and tune out the world. But I don't have that luxury. Despite the show being on hiatus, I've been swamped with publicity engagements, including one talk show after another to promote the season finale as well as my upcoming televised wedding. Many of my bookings have been with sickening Katrina. I've had to put on a happy face, play the part of Prince Charming to her Cinderella, and tell the world how excited I am to marry her while dread swims in my stomach. I wonder if Zoey's seen all the hype. It's everywhere. Katrina is the sweetheart of the media. Long live Bratrina! If only they knew.

I miss Zoey terribly. Words cannot describe what I'm going through. I miss seeing her adorable face and hearing her raspy voice. I miss every curve of her body and the touch of her soft skin in my arms. Sadly, I don't even have a photo of her. I looked online and couldn't find one. She's not on Facebook, Twitter, or Instagram, nor does she have a LinkedIn account. And when I call her cell phone, I get a message that her number is no longer in service. There's been no way to reach her. I even went around Pete and tried both Chaz and her brother. They both refused to tell me her whereabouts or give me her new number. I told Jeffrey to tell his sister that I love her. He called me a douche (which I am) and then threatened to sic the gay mafia on me if I ever got within an inch of her. Chances for that are unlikely. It's like she's fallen off the planet.

I'm bereft. It's like I'm in mourning. My big, sad, limp cock should be sheathed in a black sock. It's still attached to my shredded heart by a fragile, tethered string. With Zoey forever gone, I'm not sure if I'll ever get it up again. Or feel like a whole man.

And it's not just her heart and body I long for. I desperately need her back at my beck and call. I haven't been able to find anyone to replace her. I've been through new assistants like toilet paper. One right after another. They're either trying to get into my pants or are totally incompetent. A bunch of useless bimbos. I've missed important meetings and have been late to others because not one has been able to maintain my hectic schedule like Zoey did. Even worse, all of my social media stuff is seriously backed up. I've got ten thousand unanswered emails from fans, an equal number of Facebook messages, and I can't even begin to count the number of tweets I need to respond to. Or rather my assistant needs to reply to. It's going to be next to impossible to catch up. I fired the latest bimbo this morning after she brought me the wrong size Starbucks. I think her name was Dawn. Or was it Fawn as in fawning all over me. I can't even remember. Zoey is not only unforgettable. She's irreplaceable.

"Brandon, why aren't you ready?" Katrina's grating voice breaks into my depressing mental ramblings. Draining my Scotch, I quickly tuck Zoey's lace panties under the waistband of my sweats. No need to set the maniac off. We're having cocktails at The Four Seasons with her mother and our mutual manager Scott along with the producer and director of her reality show to go over the final wedding details. The last thing I want to do. According to Enid, the headcount is now at fifteen hundred and RSVPs are still pouring in. The big event is just two short, miserable days away. I so badly want to call the whole thing off, but the psycho bitch's threat looms. Though she acts as if nothing happened in Cannes, she slithers around me like a cobra ready to strike at any moment. The timing absolutely sucks. I owe Conquest Broadcasting my life almost as much as I owe it to my beloved Zoey. With the highly anticipated finale of *Kurt Kussler* airing on the Monday after the wedding, Blake Burns is one tightly wound up bundle of nerves. He fears Katrina is a loose stick of dynamite that can explode anytime, anywhere. And he's right.

"Jesus, Brandon, can't you answer a simple question?" Katrina's voice grows snippier as she gets closer. "What the fuck is with you lately? You sure as hell better not be having second thoughts."

"Just leave me alone, Katrina."

"Aren't we in a mood?" she snaps. Wearing her usual stilettos and a short halter-neck dress, she stops to admire herself in a mirror. Gucci, newly groomed for the wedding, catches sight of me and jumps out of her arms. He skedaddles onto the couch and cuddles next to me.

Not even the adorable pup can get me out of my funk. Nothing can. Not a swim. Not a hike. Not even a bottle of Scotch. I'm as depressed as I am stressed. Goddamn accident. Goddamn Katrina. My mind is confused; my cock is confused; and my heart is confused. I'm totally fucked up.

Katrina's sharp voice breaks once more into my thoughts. "You should get yourself a massage."

Ping. A light bulb turns on in my dark, muddled mind. Just like I'd seen them pictured in the Sunday funnies when I was a kid. I have a bright idea. For a change, Katrina's right.

"Brandon," she barks again, "let's go for God's sake."

"Katrina, why don't you head out? I have to make a few calls. I'll catch up with you and your mother shortly."

Gathering Gucci into her monstrous designer bag, she narrows her eyes and huffs. "Fine. Don't be too late. Mommy hates tardiness."

As soon as she leaves, I text my latest assistant with an assignment. After twenty frustrating minutes, she texts me back saying she's had no luck.

Keep trying.

Can't.

WTF?

I have a date with my girlfriend. See ya.

Jesus. I thought a gay assistant would be my answer. Someone who would have no interest in me physically and be willing to work 24/7. With rage blazing on my fingertips, I text her back.

YOU'RE FIRED!

To add insult to injury, she sends me a happy face emoticon. :)

Fuck. I've got to do things myself. Luck. After just one call, things are looking up.

Chapter 10

Zoey

"That was fucking amazing," says my client, a paunchy fifty-something Hollywood type named Sheldon. His privates draped by a sheet, he sits up slowly and throws his hairy, veined legs over the edge of the table. Rolls of fat spread across his ungainly torso. The fragrant lavender body oil I've rubbed him down with has only minimized the stench of his perspiration. And his fart. Adjusting his tacky comb-over across his sweaty scalp, he leers at me hungrily with his lustful eyes.

"Sweetheart, did anyone ever tell you, you're sexy?"

Only one man ever has ever had told me that. A beautiful man I'm trying hard to forget.

"No," I sputter, my heart clenching at the memory of my time in Cannes with him. "I just want to eat you up alive, you sexy little beast," Brandon said to me, holding me in his loving arms in the warm Mediterranean. Sheldon's salacious voice cuts the heart-wrenching flashback short.

"Well, gorgeous, let me tell you, you are. Whatcha doin' later?"

The gold wedding band on his ring finger has not been lost on me. Womanizing bastard! I bet he cheats on his wife all the time. She's probably one of those blond, aging big-boobed types who hang around because of the extravagant lifestyle he offers and looks the other way. He disgusts me. Makes my skin crawl.

I scoff at him. "Sorry. I've got a date with my boyfriend."

The sleazeball is hardly affected. He gives me a lecherous smile that I want to rip off his slimy face. "Maybe next time, sweetheart. And by the way, do you do private massages? You know…"

I *do* know. He wants me to give him a testicular massage and beat off his cock. I so badly want to tell him to get the hell out of here and never come back, but I bite down on my tongue and cut him off. "Sorry, I don't do private appointments. If you don't mind, would you kindly get dressed? I have to get ready for my next client."

"Sweetheart, you don't know what you're missing out on." Eyeing me lasciviously, he hoists himself off the table and hands me a five-dollar bill. The fucker.

He's also a cheap bastard! I slip it into a pocket of my clinical white uniform and mumble thank you. While he gets dressed, I step out of the small windowless room and amble to a nearby sink area to wash my hands. Thank goodness, the soap is antibacterial. I squirt a generous amount on my palms and scrub them vigorously under the hottest water I can tolerate. It's like I'm washing off cooties. If I had the time, I'd take a shower. Wash off every filthy ounce of him.

When I return to the massage room, he's gone. Donning a pair of latex gloves, I remove the sheet on the table, throw it into the hamper, and then re-drape the table with a fresh, clean one for my next client. All I know is his name is Dick Long. He's coming from another appointment—a scrub—so the aesthetician is walking him to me. I hope he's not like my previous client. But with a name like Dick Long, I wonder. Being a masseuse comes with a few plusses and a whole lot of minuses. It can be both physically and mentally draining—so many clients blabber on about their issues as if I'm their shrink while others like Sheldon come on to me. It's far from glamorous. Being cooped up in a small massage room all day is not my idea of fun. I don't know how long I'll last here, but for now it helps make ends meet and has let me continue with my acting classes, which I adore. In addition to learning so much, I've met a nice bunch of aspiring young actors like myself. There's even one guy who I think is kind of cute in a Jonah Hill kind of way and who seems to have a crush on me. His name is Albert. He even asked me out on a date for tonight. And I said yes. Progress.

A tap at the door brings me back to the present. My next client is here. My last one for the evening—it was a last-minute appointment. Scurrying over to the door, I swing it open. My heart practically stops and my knees wobble. I'm going to vomit.

"Zoey, this is your next client...Dick Long. He's booked for a two-hour deep tissue massage," says my lovely Asian colleague Esther, who, though blind, possesses renowned, magical hands.

Padding off with taps of her long white cane that can't drown out my frantic heartbeat, she leaves me alone with him. I can't get my mouth to move. I'm in a state of shock. All the air has left my lungs. I could possibly swoon.

It's Brandon. All six-feet two of his manly perfection. We're face to face, a strangled breath apart.

"Hi," he says softly, fidgeting with the belt of his long white spa robe.

A painful tangle of emotions assaults me. I blink my eyes several times, not sure if I'm going to burst into tears or explode with anger. Finally, I get my mouth to move and I do the latter.

"What are you doing here?"

"Zoey, I had to see you." He attempts to put his

hands on my shoulders, but I hastily shove them away.

"Don't you dare touch me."

His eyes flutter. He looks taken aback. "I need a massage."

"How the hell did you find me?"

"It wasn't easy. Your father wouldn't tell me nor would your brother. But I had a hunch. So I had my new assistant call every spa and massage joint in town. And then *I* found you."

"Then she's doing a good job." A sickening feeling fills my chest. I've been replaced. I was replaceable. Doormats are a dime a dozen.

"Actually, she didn't work out." His violet eyes burn into mine. "Zoey, I want you back."

Tears threaten. "So you can use and abuse me again?"

"Zoey, I didn't mean to—"

"Break my heart?" I hurl the words at him.

"I've come to apologize. I never meant to hurt you."

"Oh, it was accidental? Maybe with your amnesia, you forgot people have feelings?"

"I do have feelings toward you."

"You could have fooled me. You're some actor."

"I swear to God, Zoey, I wasn't acting. Everything I said and did with you was real."

My eyes begin to sting. Rage is rising. "You and Katrina are two delusional peas in a pod. You belong together."

"I can't leave her." He pauses for a sharp breath. "It's complicated."

That word again. A sorry excuse for an explanation.

"I have no choice. If I don't marry her on Saturday, she's threatened to say some horrific things about me to the press that could have dire consequences."

My blood boils. His words make me sure that all the things he did to me he's done to her. "Don't you have all your submissives sign confidentiality agreements?"

Brandon's face darkens. "She's not my sub. Far from it."

"Right, she's your fiancée. Have you forgotten?" My harsh voice is dripping with sarcasm.

"Zoey, I swear she means nothing to me. I despise her. It's only you. I think about you every minute of the day. You're in my blood. You're in my dreams. You have no idea how hard it's been for me."

His voice is cracking with emotion. He sounds sincere. And despair is etched on his gorgeous as ever face. I quickly remind myself he's an actor. A great actor. Don't fall for his bullshit, I will myself.

Rage crescendos inside me. "Brandon, stop feeding me this crap. Did they ever teach you in acting classes that actions speak louder than words?"

Without warning, he shoves me against a wall, pinning me against it with his hips and gripping my shoulders so tightly I wince. His body is so close to mine I feel the heat of his skin and smell the scent of his sex. My breasts compress against his iron chest, my nipples stiffening as he nuzzles my neck. I'm more aroused than a dog in heat.

"What are you fucking doing?" I cry out.

"Zoey, you've touched me everywhere, but the place you've touched me deepest is here."

Still pinning me to the wall, he cinches my right arm by the wrist and slips my hand between us, pressing it hard against his heart. I feel it pound beneath my palm. Perhaps, I should tell him to feel my heart. The shattered chambers. The shards.

"Let me go, you asshole!" I beg instead.

His mouth responds with a crashing, fiery kiss that blazes through me. Oh my God. I want him. No, I don't. Yes, I do! This cruel game with a burning tightrope has no safety net. It threatens to destroy me. His rigid length singes my flesh right through his robe and my clothes. A ring of fire circles my core, and the white-hot heat radiates from my head to my toes. I succumb to the urgency of his mouth on mine with a moan.

He bites down on my lower lip, parting it, and then plunges his warm tongue inside my mouth, sweeping across the vessel, deepening the kiss with my submission. His other hand slips beneath the waistband of my uniform and makes its way to my wetness, caressing my slick cleft and aching clit. Flames lick my skin. I wriggle beneath his weight and moan louder. Oh God!

What the fuck am I doing? Why am I letting him do these things to me? Unable to resist, I squeeze my eyes shut until I'm seeing stars.

Finally, he pulls his scorching lips away and releases my right hand. "Oh baby, I want you so fucking badly," he breathes into my mouth. "More than anything."

The words on my tongue waver between "Fuck you" and "Fuck me." Taking a deep tormented breath, I do something I've never done before. I slap him hard across his face, leaving my handprint on his cheek and an echo in my ear. He rubs his stubble-lined jaw while I rub my stinging palm.

Tears scald the back of my eyes. "That's all you're getting from me. Whatever sick, cruel game you're playing, Brandon, needs to end. I let you take everything. My heart. My soul. My body. My mind. But the one thing you're not going to take is the last ounce of my dignity."

"I'm sorry, Zoey. I couldn't help myself."

Neither could I.

"Zo, just give me a massage. That's all. I need to feel your beautiful hands on me." His voice is thick with desperation. And his eyes glint with despair. "I've already paid for your services."

My heart clenches so tightly it hurts. "Oh, so, you think I'm some kind of whore?"

"Jeez, Zoey, no!"

"Go to hell!" I choke out the words. "I'm no longer at your command. You're not my boss and I have the right to refuse anyone."

"Oh, is that in your contract?" His tone sharpening, he makes air quotes around the word "contract." With all my willpower, I hold my own.

"Either you leave or I leave."

"Zoey, please."

Please. Mama taught me to say that word. "*Please, Brandon, I just want to forget you.*"

"Zoey—"

"Brandon, PLEASE. I never want to see you again." I'm a titanic mess, yet I so want my heart to go on.

Brandon's jaw slackens in near defeat. I need to strike like a snake while I can.

"And just for your information, I have a real boy-friend now. Someone who's normal...who treats me with kindness and respect."

That sadistic satanic expression sweeps over him. His face darkens. "I'm happy for you, Zoey. But does he fuck you the way I do?"

"He doesn't fuck *with* me the way you do."

Silence. His nostrils flare.

"He loves me," I lie.

Tears verging, I grab my bag. I've got to escape. The air is suffocating me. He's suffocating me. Drowning me, pulling me under. I'll just tell my supervisor I fell sick. It's way closer to the truth than a lie.

"No, Zoey! Don't go," he growls, clutching my waist so tightly I yelp. I struggle to free myself like a wild animal captured by a poacher.

"Let me go!" I cry out, writhing and flailing, clawing and gnawing, batting him with my bag. We exchange savage sounds. And expletives. Overpowering me with his strength, he lifts me off my feet and flings me onto the massage table face up. I bolt to a sitting position, but he shoves me flat down on my back and then straddles me. His powerful knees hold me captive while he throws off his robe. Before it hits the floor, his large bruising hands grip my shoulders, holding me down. He leans into me, so close his breath heats my cheeks and I can taste him. His face is just inches away. His jet-black hair, longer and wilder, falls into his smoldering violet eyes. They're filled with mad lust and desire. My blood pounds in my ears with each beat of my heart as I fight back my dire need for him to possess me.

"Give yourself to me, Zoey."

"Fuck you, bastard."

His eyes narrow. "You're asking for it."

I am. I want him to fuck me so badly it hurts.

With an angry grunt, he forcefully spreads my legs and yanks down my pants, taking my panties with them. He grabs my soaked crotch and squeezes a fistful of pussy. His eyes hold me fiercely. I'm a willing prisoner of his beauty, his supreme masculinity. I drink in his broad shoulders, sculpted pecs, rippled abs, muscled limbs, and the taut bronzed flesh aglow from the scrub that ties all the parts together. My hands want to touch him everywhere.

He squeezes my cleft harder, rolling his thumb around my throbbing nub. Moaning, I feel myself getting hotter, wetter with each powerful stroke. Pulsing electrical heat spirals through every ounce of my being until I'm burning with desire, every cell on fire. My mind fights for control, but my feverish body betrays me, craving him deep between my thighs.

"Oh, my beautiful Zoey, you're so fucking hot and wet for me. I have to have you." His voice has grown demanding. The warmth of his breath against my flesh takes my breath away. My breathing grows shallow as he continues to arouse me.

"Tell me you want me as much I want you."

His irresistible magnetic energy draws me to him, making it impossible to say no. Biting down on my lips to stifle a scream, I nod, wanting him as much as he wants me. Maybe more.

"Zoey, I need to hear words."

"Oh, God!" It's all I can manage.

"You're mine. Do you hear me? You're mine!" With his other hand, he fists the base of his enormous cock. A bead of pre-cum dots the crown like a shimmering pearl. His rock-hard monument to mankind is as beautiful as I remember. Magnificent. A vision of incomparable virile perfection.

"Say you want me," he repeats, "and that you're mine. Do it…please."

That very word is on the tip of my tongue, but my mouth won't release it. *Please… fuck me. Fuck me hard. Fuck me now.* My chest heaves. I tremble with all the love and hate I feel for this man. The tremors ransack my melting body. I hate myself for wanting him when having him is not a reality.

Not waiting for my response, his massive cock presses against my entrance like a hot rock massage. At the touch of it, I arch, wanting him to fill me, to take me completely with all of his sublimity. With one long, forceful thrust, he rams into me, taking me to the hilt. *Oh God, yes!!* I moan with the burst of exquisite pain that equals in measure to my anguish at the sensation of his raging erection inside me. Anchoring his hands on either side of me, he begins to pummel me without mercy, cursing under his ragged breaths. Meeting his thrusts with my hips, I sob for all I remember and for all I want to forget. The agony and the ecstasy. The love and the hate. As I ready to climax, a voice inside my head rises above my wails.

STOP! No, Zoey, No. I can't let him do this to me. Make me fall apart. Shatter an already shattered heart. I call upon all the willpower I can muster. *Zoey, be strong.* Mind over matter, I find my voice.

One word. My voice so soft, it's almost a prayer. "Mama."

It happens so fast. On my next heartbeat, he releases me, withdrawing without a word. His violet eyes are glazed and forlorn, like an addict who can't get his fix. He dismounts the table. With his darkening orbs on me, I sit up and pull up both my pants and panties. My eyes stay steady on his tortured face.

Sliding off the table, I walk away. And then run.

Chapter 11

Brandon

I kissed her like it was our last kiss. And likely it was. And fucked her like a mad man as if there was no tomorrow. What the fuck was I thinking? With a red-hot mixture of rage and regret, I bang the roof of my Lamborghini so hard I've likely left a dent both in it and my wrist. I wince. Fuck. Shit. Fuck. She's over me. She gave me a slap instead of her heart. And to add insult to injury, spit out her safe word. She's moved on. Fallen in love with someone else. She must be happy. She looked so beautiful, her complexion radiant, her body fit though a little too thin.

As if the first bang isn't bad enough. I bang the roof again. God dammit, I totally fucked up. I couldn't help it. The second I laid my eyes on her I grew as hard as nails and had the burning need to bury my cock deep inside her...completely possess her. Then, when she told me about her boyfriend, I went crazy with jealousy and totally lost control. With my cock raging like a bull, I tried to fuck her into submission when I should have told her what really happened in Cannes. *And* then told her I loved her. Never an ad libber, I suck at love unscripted. My deflated, aching cock berates me. *Stupid idiot.* She was right. I'm a bastard. A fucking bastard. Actually, I'm worse than that. I'm a coward. A spineless coward who's afraid to speak his mind and fight for what he wants, no matter what the consequences of his words and actions will be.

With my hand throbbing almost as much as my cock, I tear out of the underground parking garage and zoom down Crescent Heights. My engine roaring, I run every red light, not knowing where the fuck I'm heading. Horns blast at me from every direction, and I'm surprised a cop doesn't pull me over. I turn on the radio as loud as it gets, and a remix of Nick Jonas's "Jealous" booms in my ears. Yes, Zoey's too sexy, beautiful and I'm never going to get another taste of her. If the car's speeding at eighty miles an hour, my heart's racing at eight hundred. My life is so fucking out of control.

Running yet another red light, I impulsively make a sharp turn onto Wilshire, still not knowing where the hell I'm going. *Screech!* I lose control of the wheel and the car swerves to the right, skidding off the road. I hold my foot tight on the brake as the screeching car careens into one of those modernist condo complexes that are popping up all over town. *CRASH!* My head bangs against the steering wheel before the monstrous airbag detonates in my face with the explosive sound of a gunshot. The smell of smoke and gunpowder infiltrates my dazed, aching head.

"Dude, are you okay?" An unfamiliar adolescent voice drifts into my ears.

I can't get my voice box to respond. I think I've lost consciousness. Or I'm in shock.

"Want me to call for an ambulance?"

With a moan, I slowly lift my head from the deflated airbag. It's spread out like a parachute, the edges frayed and singed, the middle bloodied. My eyes half-shut, I painfully twist my neck and peer out the open window. A scruffy kid, clutching a skateboard, meets my gaze. His eyes widen and his jaw drops. He recognizes me.

"Shit, man. Aren't you—"

I cut him off. "No."

Not convinced, the kid knits his brows. "Whoever you are, you're bleeding. You sure you don't want me to call 911?"

"Please don't," I mumble.

"Want me to help you out?"

"No. Stand back." Praying that the fancy switch-blade doors haven't jammed, I hit a button on my dashboard. To my relief, they lift up as the wide-eyed kid watches in awe. A loud "wow" flies out of his mouth.

Using all the strength I have, I slide out of the car and stagger to my feet. My head is killing me so badly I'm dizzy. I feel warm blood trickle down my cheek.

Holding on to the roof for balance, I survey the damage. The hood's crushed like an accordion and the engine's smoking like a chimney. My precious one hundred thousand dollar Lambo may be totaled. But you know what? I don't care.

"Mister—"

Ignoring the concerned kid and the cluster-fuck, I start walking. One painful step after another. There's someone I need to see.

It takes me forty-five long, desperate, desolate minutes to get to my destination by foot. It should have taken only twenty, but I'm unable to walk in a straight line or take strong, steady steps. Plus, I take side streets to avoid pedestrians in my pitiful state. If I pass one, I just bow my head, skirting their gaze. A nanny with a stroller comes at me from around a corner and, with one glimpse, scurries past me, her expression one of pure terror. With my swollen, blood-streaked face and stained, ragged T-shirt, I must look frightening. As the sun descends and the pink-flecked sky morphs into an orange-blue hue, fewer people take notice of me. A dog-walker ignores me. Dusk is my friend.

Bella's cottage is on Spaulding, a charming, palm tree lined street in Beverly Hills south of Wilshire. It's not the über-mansion Beverly Hills of the rich and famous, but rather a middle-class neighborhood, filled with modest one-family stucco homes and duplexes, many built in the twenties. A rose garden and beds of colorful flowers line the verdant lawn. While not large, her beautifully lit, pink-stucco one-story house has incredible curb appeal. Taking a deep breath, I eschew the bell and knock at the wood door. Seven rapid times in succession. The way I signaled my arrival at her doorstep many years ago when I was her student.

Almost instantly, a trim, brown-skinned woman with twinkling dark eyes and wearing the uniform of a professional caretaker, comes to the door and swings it open. She looks to be from India or Pakistan. Masking any shock at my gruesome appearance, she leads me through the entryway to the coved-ceiling living room. It's exactly as I remember it. Filled with worn vintage velvet furnishings draped with fringed silk shawls, oriental rugs scattered on dark hardwood floors, and whimsical bronze lamps with hand-painted glass shades that bathe the rose-colored walls in a warm amber glow. Scented candles are everywhere and soft classical music fills the air.

No, the house hasn't changed a bit, but she has. My

bleary eyes drink her in. She was always twenty-five-years older than me, but then her beauty negated the age difference. Though still stunning, she now looks older than her years. She's let her long ebony hair turn silver and her thinness has given way to gauntness. Crinkly gray eyes set off her high cheekbones, which against the hollows of her cheeks look like apples. The woman, who would be bent over the couch, naked with her gorgeous ass in the air, always ready for me, is now hunched in a wheelchair. A blanket covers her withered legs. She shakes. And upon seeing me, her tremors become more pronounced. She has Parkinson's.

"Divya," she says in her still breathy, deep theatrical voice, "please bring me my first aid kit, an ice pack, and a glass of water with some Advil."

"Right away, Miss Stadler." The exotic caretaker scuttles off.

"Brandon, come here," she orders, her voice softer.

Battling fatigue and pain, I take one small shaky step after another in her direction, each step more agonizing than the one before. It feels like an eternity until I reach her and when I do, I fall to my knees and bury my face in her lap. I do something I've done only once—when my parents died—I cry.

A melodic "shh" sounds in my ears. Her fingertips caress my scalp while I heave quietly and shed tears into her soft cashmere blanket. I seek solace with the extraordinary woman who taught me to master my craft and master my sexuality. The teacher who introduced me to the world of BDSM and taught me to be a Dom.

The lifestyle she introduced me to felt so right. So out of control after my parents' demise, the control I got from sexual domination filled a need, a void. She was the perfect teacher. The perfect submissive. Strong but compliant. Vulnerable but fearless. A willing sub to indulge in the pain I inflicted and the pleasure I gave her. She showed me all kinds of kinks and fetishes, and opened my mind and body to fantasies and desires, blurring the line between acting out our fantasies and satisfying our real needs. A classically trained pianist, she compared our sexploits to Mozart. Just the way he included unexpected little notes and trills in his music to make the piece twinkle and feel more fun, our trills were composed of spankings, candle wax, sex toys, and much more. We had boundaries and she had a safe word, Shakespeare, but her hard limits were limited. She opened my eyes; she opened my world. As much as I needed to be a Dom, she needed to be a sub and relinquish the control she exerted in her everyday life over her academy and students. Shut down her brain and let me make the choices. Surrender. It was the perfect Dom-sub relationship. And then she got sick.

I don't know how long I stay in this position when I hear her voice again.

"Mr. Taylor, look up at me."

Wordlessly, I lift my head and meet her gaze.

"What happened?" Her husky submissive voice is soft.

"I fucked up. I crashed my car."

Her prescient eyes penetrate mine. "What *really* happened?"

Before I can answer, Divya returns with a silver tray full of first aid items and a bag of ice.

"Divya, please set the tray down on the end table and give us some time alone together."

"Yes, ma'am," says the obliging caretaker.

"And would you please make us some tea."

Divya quietly departs.

With her frail, trembling hands, Bella opens the bottle of peroxide and moistens a cotton ball. She dabs it on my gash. Still in a kneeling position, I wince.

"Shit. That hurts."

A small smile lifts her lips. "You, better than anyone, know that pain comes with healing."

And then pleasure.

"Press this against the wound," she commands after cleaning up my blood-caked cheeks.

She lifts my hand to my face, and nursing my open cut, I watch as she soaks another ball with the antiseptic liquid. One more dab, this one not as stingy, and then she lightly kisses the wound. Not so much as a lover, but rather as a mother kissing a child's scraped knee. I close my eyes and let out a grateful moan. Reopening them, my gaze stays on her as she struggles to open the box of Band-Aids with her trembling fingers. I have the burning urge to help her but know that small gesture will humiliate her. Despite being my sub, she relished her independence. After a few tries, she opens the lid and then fishes for the right size bandage with her long slender fingers, still so elegant though now withered and quivering. They remind me so much of Zoey's.

"Don't move," she tells me. She peels off the wrapping and places the bandage over my wound. She admires her handiwork.

"Well, Brandon, I must say you look a lot like a battered Marlon Brando in *On the Waterfront*— although a hell of a lot more handsome." She pauses to smile. "Now put the ice pack to your face."

I reach for the ice pack and press it against my forehead. Ahh! Pain followed by pleasure. The coldness of the compress soothes my raw skin. With my free hand, I reach for the Advil and flush a couple tablets down my throat with a few sips of water.

Divya returns with another silver tray, this one holding a floral tea service. Setting the tray down on the glass coffee table, she pours two cups of tea. One for Bella, one for me. I stand and then sit on the edge of the couch, close to her wheelchair.

"Divya dear, please put two lumps of sugar into Mr. Taylor's tea and one into mine." She remembers how I like it. I put the hot, fragrant brew to my mouth with my free hand, and as I take a small sip, memories flood my mind. It was fittingly over the play, *Tea and Sympathy*, the story of a forbidden teacher-student romance, that our relationship transcended the normal teacher-student bond. It turned sexual. She, the older, wiser, more experienced teacher of a lifestyle that transformed my life. We couldn't get enough of each other.

Once, ice packs and hot tea bags brought us to orgasmic heights, the dual sensations of each playing off one another until she could no longer bear it and I couldn't wait for her to come. While memories abound of our outrageous sexcapades, my eyes stay fixed on her as she slowly lifts her porcelain cup to her lips with her shaky hand. Still always pinky out. Erect as a cock. She blows on the steamy greenish liquid before taking a sip. Her still sensuous pursed lips remind me of how many times they kissed me everywhere, lighting the fire and desires of a fucked-up eighteen-year-old kid who almost overdosed on heroin. I owe her my career. I owe her my life.

"Thank you for the tea," I say after taking another soothing sip.

She smiles at me warmly again. "It's a special Ayurvedic blend from India composed of magical herbs that help balance one's doshas and hence keep the body and mind in harmony. It restores your body's natural ability to heal itself."

The tea is exactly what I need, but I doubt it can heal the hole in my heart. Nothing can, except one unattainable human being.

After another sip, she sets the cup down on its saucer. She strokes my face. "You know, I watch your show every week."

"You do?" I never knew that. "What do you think?"

"Of the show? Or of you?"

I quirk a nervous smile, knowing she never holds back. "Both."

"You deserved to win the Golden Globe. And so did the series."

"You watched?"

"Of course. Thank you for acknowledging me."

Silently grateful that Zoey reminded me to include her in my acceptance speech, I smile a genuine smile— the first since she ran away from me in Cannes. "Bella, you made me both the actor and man I am."

"That was my job. You're the best student I ever had." She pauses to take another sip of tea. "And the best lover."

Never married, Bella had many. But to the best of my knowledge, she never took on another after me. She eyes me warmly.

"And thank you for the generous donation to my school. It allowed me to give a scholarship to a lovely young woman whose talent rivals yours. I have high hopes for her."

While she now only occasionally shows up for auditions or a guest lecture because of her debilitating degenerative disease, she still runs the academy with an iron fist. Over the years, I've contributed several million dollars that's enabled her to open other branches around the country, maintain the facilities, and offer scholarships to talented kids, like the girl she mentioned, who can't afford the tuition.

"The money comes from my heart."

"It means a lot to me." She changes the subject. "So, I hear you're getting married to that awful woman who *thinks* she's America's It Girl."

My brows arch. It hurts to lift them. "You've met her?"

"Yes. I had the misfortune of meeting her at the hospital when I came to visit you after your horrible hit and run back in January. She and that despicable manager of yours forbid me from seeing you."

Rage rips through my bloodstream. Fucking Katrina. Fucking Scott. How dare they shoo away the two most important people in my life—my beloved Zoey and my mentor Bella?

My chest tightening, I remove the melting ice pack from my head and set it back on the tray. I suck in a sharp breath. "It's fucked up. I'm not in love with her. I want to call it off."

"So, Brandon, why don't you?"

I inhale deeply again. "She's threatened to expose my kinks. Actually worse... portray me as a life-threatening sex molester even though there's never been any sex between us. I supposedly fell in love with her and proposed just before my hit and run accident, but I have no recollection."

Bella's inquisitive eyes narrow. "What do you mean?"

"I suffered amnesia. Lost ten years of my life. Just about everything's come back to me except my time with her and the actual day of the accident." Over another sip of the hot tea, I pause. "I'm sick about the whole thing. I don't want to marry her."

Looking up at the ceiling, Bella dreamily lowers her eyelids. "For, as a surfeit of the sweetest things…"

Shakespeare. *A Midsummer Night's Dream.* I remember the lines as if I recited them yesterday. I played Lysander, the foolish young man who deceives his true love, Hermia.

"…the deepest loathing to the stomach brings. Or as the heresies that men do leave are hated most of those they did deceive. So thou, my surfeit and my heresy, of all be hated, but the most of me!"

Nodding, Bella meets my gaze. "There's someone else, isn't there?"

I blink twice. "How do you know?"

"My beloved Brandon, people are an open book. I'm trained to read sensory, physical, and psychological cues. Your emotions are written all over you. They read like a man madly in love."

"I am." I swallow the two little words.

"Who might this person be?"

"My assistant. Or should I say former assistant. I love all of her. Everything about her."

"She loves you?"

"I thought she did. But now I'm not sure. I screwed up big time. She's shut me out and wants nothing to do with me."

"The course of true love never did run smooth."

One of Shakespeare's most famous lines and oh so fitting. I feel like I've been dragged through a raging river, encountering every jagged rock along the way.

"Brandon, would you please wheel me around so I'm facing you."

Standing up, I do as asked. Once again, I feel like her student in the classroom of life.

"Please sit back down."

I do as bid, and so close to me, she holds my face between her frail, shaking hands. They're icy cold and feel good on my fiery skin. Her warm breath heats my chilled bones. Our eyes lock.

"Mr. Taylor, you're not here just for tea and sympathy."

"Bella, I'm lost. I don't know what to do."

"What did I always tell you to do in my classes?"

The words whirl around my head. "Act with your heart."

"Yes. And what else did I insist on you doing?"

The unforgettable, very first words of my mentor

pour out of my mouth. "Don't follow your dreams. Lead them and land them."

"Yes. Do it, Brandon. Do it."

A rush of love for this incredible woman surges inside me. Not like a gush of hot lava the way it used to, but more like a sprinkle of refreshing water wanting to give life to a withering rose. She's still irresistible. My lips are about to touch down on hers when her caretaker reappears. The chinoiserie grandfather's clock in the corner starts chiming.

"I'm sorry, Mr. Taylor, you must leave now. It's Miss Stadler's bedtime."

I nod. Bella, still cupping my jaw, submits to my lips, and we both lose ourselves in a soft, tender kiss. Not the kiss of two lovers but rather of two souls connected forever. I know in my heart it'll be our last. On the final, ninth chime of the clock, we break away. Her soulful eyes hold mine.

"I don't have much time, Brandon. Make yourself happy. Make me proud."

Chapter 12

Zoey

I was only half-lying to Brandon. I do have a boyfriend. Well, sort of. He's someone from my acting class who's been crushing on me. After we performed a scene from Shakespeare's *A Midsummer Night's Dream* in which he played Puck, the bumbling love fairy, to my lead of the jilted heroine Hermia, he built up the courage to ask me to lunch at the Greek deli next door. And I said yes.

His name is Albert Schwimmer. Maybe because he's on the chubby side, I can't help thinking of *Fat Albert*. That cartoon series.

"Why did your parents name you Albert?" I asked right after our order was delivered to the table.

After biting into his overstuffed, greasy gyro sandwich, he responded, "They thought it would make me smart. Like Albert Einstein."

I almost choked on my low-cal veggie burger. "That's one of the funniest things I've ever heard."

He laughed back and then asked me out on a real date...

Tonight of all nights, right after my emotionally devastating encounter with Brandon. Sick to my stomach, I've thought about canceling it. Saying I have Ebola. Which, with the way I feel, is almost true. But after much deliberation, I decide not to. A new person in my life might be the best medicine to cure me of my real, potentially fatal disease. The disease that's ravaging both my body and my heart. Brandonitis.

Still tasting him and wearing the intoxicating scent of him, I eschew a shower, unable to wash him away. I hastily throw on some clothes. Albert is taking me bowling at a nearby bowling alley in Hollywood. So jeans, sneakers, and a sweatshirt—my *Kurt Kussler* one—will suffice.

While I haven't done it in ages, I love to bowl. Pops is in a league and he started me out at an early age. Bowling helped me funnel my anger toward Mama's murderer. When I hurled that big ball down the long, narrow lane, I fantasized striking him down. It really helped me with my game.

At seven p.m. sharp, a horn honks outside my window. Taking a final glimpse of my pathetic self in the mirror, I trudge downstairs from my second-floor apartment. Albert's gray Toyota Corolla is waiting for me outside. I hop in.

Bowling should be fun, but tonight it's not and I'm off my game. Distracted, I can't get my mind off Brandon. He totally unraveled me and reactivated every physical and emotional feeling I have for him. It was bad enough just seeing him, but when he kissed me, that's all it took for me to succumb. The touch of his lips on mine melted me, turned every bone in my body into molten liquid. If he hadn't pinned me against a wall, I would have crumbled. And then I let him ravish me on the massage table until somehow I found the strength inside me to make him stop before he made me fall apart again. It was bad enough putting the pieces of myself back together the first time and I knew I could never do it again. Yet, here I am once again, a total train wreck.

With a forceful swing, I hurl my last bowling ball down the glistening lane. My eyes stay fixed on it as it rolls smack down the middle at a dizzying speed. *KABOOM!* The ball rams into the pins, knocking all but one down.

While I wait for the ball to return, I narrow my eyes at the sole pin that's standing at the very far right. The erect pin challenges me. And suddenly it has a face. Brandon's! Fuck you, asshole! My purple bowling ball comes back to me. Curling my fingers into the three holes, I toss it down the alley with as much force as I can muster. My gaze never wavers from it as it speeds down the lane and knocks down the lone pin with a POW. A spare.

"Wow! You're amazing!" says Albert. "You won! How'd you learn to bowl like that?"

One of Pops's mottos comes to mind. "Practice makes perfect," I say glumly as I realize my victory. Final score: One hundred fifty to Albert's gutter-driven ninety.

I should be elated, but I'm not. My heart's way heavier than my lucky ball.

After a quick bite—chilidogs which I barely touched—we're back at my Beachwood Canyon apartment complex. Albert parks his car in front of it. We share a short awkward silence and then he breaks it.

"Can I come up?' His bespectacled eyes stayed glued on me.

Another tense moment. After much deliberation, I say, "Sure." Regret immediately sets in.

"Cool digs," he says, taking in my small apartment five minutes later.

"It's okay." I shrug. "Want a glass of wine? Or a beer?"

"You got milk?"

Milk? "Yeah, sure. I'll be right back."

When I return to the living room with a glass of milk in hand, Albert's nowhere to be found. Maybe he's split. No such luck.

"Cool beans," I hear him shout out. His voice is

coming from my bedroom.

Upon entering it, my jaw drops to the floor. Fat Albert has taken off his pants and polo shirt and is now clad only in his Superman briefs. A big red and yellow insignia "S" lines up with his cock while a major pair of love handles hangs over the waistband.

"Here's your milk," I say, keeping my eyes on his face as I hand it to him.

"Thanks." He gulps it down and then sets the glass on my dresser. A white mustache lines his upper lip, and I can't help but think of that famous ad campaign, "Got milk?" I wish I hadn't.

He burps.

Still wearing his horn-rimmed glasses, he stares at my *Kurt Kussler* poster, which is leaning against the wall facing my bed. Like a kid in a candy store, drooling and in awe. A comforting thought. Maybe he's gay, but then I remember men love Kurt. They long to be the devastating action hero.

"Wowee cowzowzee! You have a signed poster of *Kurt Kussler*!" Albert gushes. "How'd you get it?"

"I found it at a garage sale," I lie.

"Lucky you! He's amazing!"

"Yeah." So *fucking* amazing.

"Do you watch the show?"

"Sometimes," I stammer.

"I can't wait to see the season finale. It's going to be a killer."

"Maybe I'll try to catch it." My lackluster voice masks the torrent of emotions coursing through me.

"Man, no one can act like Brandon Taylor."

"No one can act like a bigger asshole than Brandon Taylor" is what I want to say, but instead I say he's just okay.

"Just okay? C'mon. He's fucking unbelievable. That dude could recite the phone book and win an award. I wish I could be as good as him."

No one can be as good as him. Not only can he act better than anyone, he can also sing like a rock star. That unforgettable night in Cannes seeps into my brain. Dancing in his arms as he sang Mama's favorite song. Pressing my fingertips to my temples, I try to make the memory disappear from my mind. It's impossible. He's unforgettable in every way.

"Are you okay?" asks Albert.

I nod. "Yeah. Just a bit of a headache. I had a hard day at work." A *really* hard day. Avoiding eye contact with anything below his shoulders, I focus on my companion.

"Albert, you shouldn't be so tough on yourself. You're very talented."

His eyes light up. "Really? You think so?"

"Yes. I've seen you in class. You've got great co-medic timing."

He grins. "I bet Brandon could do comedy. He can do everything."

Yes, he could make me laugh as much as cry. And sometimes he made me laugh so hard I was crying. Like the time he couldn't get his fly down with his sprained fingers and the night he made me sleep with him in my pajamas with little Gucci. All the fun, sexy moments we shared dance in my head—from our first sensual shower, both fully clothed, to that delicious bath in Cannes that ended it all. Albert's nasal voice cuts into my beautiful but excruciating memories.

"Are you going to watch him get married to that reality star, Katrina Moore, this weekend?"

My heart clenches and my stomach churns. Their televised wedding is just two days away. I falter for an excuse. "Um, uh, no. I don't own a TV."

"You can watch it with me," Albert says brightly.

"I-I don't think so. I don't like reality shows." The truth: I can't face the reality of Brandon marrying her. Or the pain. I inhale and exhale as if it's my last breath.

"Albert, can we please change the subject?"

Albert leers at me. "Can we talk about your poonani?"

My poonani? "Excuse me. What's that?"

"You know. Your vagina."

I gulp while he rubs his dick with his hand.

"Superman would really like to get to know it."

Gah! He calls his cock Superman. My eyes shoot down. Maybe it's super big though the bulge in his cotton briefs doesn't suggest that.

Before I can say a word, he starts fondling me. His touch is nothing like Brandon's. He's touching me in all the wrong places, and he's doing nothing to arouse me. I feign a moan. Acting 101.

"Zoey, you're very appealing." He lifts his glasses to the top of his head, and then his lips collide with mine like a bad car accident. Mentally, I wish I'd swerved off course or put my brakes on, but it's too late.

Ugh! His slobbering kiss tastes of milk and hot chili, and it's accompanied by snorts. He's giving my face a full-on tongue bath with his drool. I want desperately to break away. Then rinse my mouth with mouthwash and spit it all out.

Deepening the kiss, his sharp teeth scrape along my teeth. Almost as bad as nails to a chalkboard, the grating sound gives me shivers and makes the hair on the back of my neck stand on end. He's hurting me— not in a good way. Okay. Three words: Worst. Kiss. Ever.

And if that's not bad enough, Superman comes flying out. I feel his dick poke against me. All measly five inches of a semi-hard curl. Undoing my jeans, he pulls them down along with my panties just below my hips and then attempts to shove Superman into my poo-poo-poo-poo…I can't wrap my head around that word nor get my legs to spread. They're super-glued together.

"C'mon, Zoey. Open up for Superman. Let me be

your man of steel."

He keeps nudging. But I'm not wet. And I can't pry my legs apart. My wide-open eyes dart to Brandon's poster. His intense violet eyes are on me, and I can practically hear him saying his words: "Get it. Got it? Good." Nothing's good. I can't take this. Finally, I push Albert away. He stumbles, almost falling to the floor.

"Zoey, why'd you do that?"

"I'm s-sorry." *I really am.*

He looks wounded. "You're not attracted to me. You think I'm fat, right?"

I pull up my panties and jeans. "No, Albert. It's not that. I mean, look at me. I'm hardly Miss America."

His voice grows more despondent. "Is it because my pee-pee is small?"

"No, Albert. Your dick is just fine."

"Then, what is it, Zoey?" he asks, sliding up his caped crusader briefs. "I thought you liked me."

Setting his glasses back on the bridge of his nose, I run a hand through his bristly ginger hair. "Albert, I need to be honest with you. I just broke up with someone. It was very painful. It's been a month. I thought I was ready for another relationship, but I'm not."

He looks at me earnestly. "Then, maybe I can be a friend with benefits."

I shake my head. "No, Albert. You can't."

His expression grows deflated; his voice wavers.

"Just a friend?"

"Yeah. Just a friend. I'd like that."

Albert's face brightens. "Okay. Maybe it'll blossom into something bigger. I'm a patient kind of guy."

I shoot him a half-smile. "Maybe. But right now, I think you should put your pants back on and go home."

Silently, he does what I ask. My head stays bowed as he gets dressed.

"Night, Zoey." He turns on his heel.

"Albert, wait."

With a glimmer of hope, he steps up to me. I give him a small peck on his cheek.

"Thank you, Albert, for a very nice evening. I'll see you in class next week."

"Yeah…See ya." Shrugging with defeat, he lumbers toward the bedroom door.

Once I hear my front door slam shut, I slide my jeans back off and collapse onto the bed. Under the watchful eyes of Brandon Taylor, I lean back against my headboard and bend up my knees. There's a fire that's been raging all night between my thighs. I slip my hand beneath my panties, and with the scarred finger I cut when I trashed the poster, I rub my clit vigorously. My eyes stay on the poster. Wetness seeps through the cotton crotch. My heartbeat accelerates and the T-shirt beneath my sweatshirt clings to my heated chest. I rub harder and faster. Oh God! Why can't I come? Aren't my magical hands good enough anymore? I feel pressure but no pleasure. Frustrated, I jump out of bed and scurry to my dresser. I yank open the top drawer and rummage through my underwear until I find it. The vibrator I bought at the Pleasure Chest. Sparky. It's time to break it open. Frantically, I tear the plastic package apart. *Whoof!* I'm not prepared for the stench—it smells like a fifty-foot high pile of un-wrapped condoms—and hurry back to my bed before it puts me into anaphylactic shock. Resuming my bent-knee position, I switch the stinky pink vibrator on and place it between my legs so the little rabbit's ears stimulate my clit while I thrust the penis-shaped latex into my chasm. A loud buzz sounds in my ears. I feel like I'm at the dentist getting a cavity filled.

BUZZZZZZZ! I hate the buzz! I hate the way the vibrator feels. The pathetic, ticklish rabbit feels nothing like the kneading of Brandon's long magical fingers, and the vibrating latex penis thing inside me is no substitute for the exquisite sensation of his enormous, thrusting cock of velvet. I long to hear his savage grunts and groans while feeling the heat of his weight on top of me, skin-to-skin, heart-to-heart, organ to organ. Yes, savor his magnificence deep inside of me. And then hear him roar my name as I break into an epic orgasm around his explosive rock-hard length.

Screw Sparky. He's not creating any sparks. Instead of getting turned on, I'm getting turned off. In fact, I'm numb. Impetuously, I withdraw the vibrator and hurl it

at the *Kurt Kussler* poster. It narrowly misses and lands
with a clunk on the floor. Oh, God!! Why won't that
awful buzzing stop? That rabbit's like the fucking
Energizer bunny. It keeps going and going and going. I
clap my hands to my ears hoping to drown it out as a
horrible reality hits me. Brandon Taylor has ruined me
for all other men. For toys with benefits. And made me
my own worst enemy. The unbearable ache between
my legs returns with a vengeance as does the ache in
my shredded heart.

"Fuck you, Brandon!" I shout at the *Kurt Kussler*
poster, and then I cry myself to sleep.

Chapter 13

Brandon

A cab takes me back home. My head is still killing me. I should probably take another Advil, but instead I stagger to the liquor cabinet and pour myself a Scotch. I down the shot in one gulp and then pour myself another. Outside my house, I hear a car whip into the driveway. And then shortly, I hear the front door open and slam shut with a bang so loud it hurts my head. She storms into the living room, her spiky heels clickety-clacking and likely making dents on my wood floor. Fucking Katrina.

"Where the hell were you?" she barks.

Polishing off the Scotch, I turn to face her.

Her face scrunches in disgust. I'm not sure if it's at the sight of me or because she's simmering mad. I have my answer on her next blazing question.

"Why the fuck didn't you pick up your phone? I

called you a dozen times. Mommy was furious."

Any other person in their right mind would say something like: "Oh my God! What happened to you? Are you okay?" upon seeing my mess of a face. While I haven't yet taken a look at myself, the rawness of my skin and the excruciating pain behind my eyes are enough to clue me in that I look disastrous. A pang of sadness stabs me. For sure Zoey would care.

"Answer my question," she hisses.

"I got into an accident. I didn't know you called. I left my phone in my car." Balls. It's probably gotten towed. Something I'll have to deal with tomorrow—all by myself since I once again don't have an assistant. I'll probably also have to file some kind of police report. My Zoey would have taken care of everything, including my pounding headache. Draining the Scotch, I pour myself yet another shot and chug it while Katrina rants on.

"Moron. And just look at you. We're getting married in two days and you look like fricking Frankenstein."

The truth: Compared to the way I must look, Frankenstein could be *People Magazine's* "Sexiest Man Alive." I rub my throbbing head. My headache's getting worse, and I'm not sure if it's because of my injury, the Scotch, or a combination of both—or maybe just breathing in toxic Katrina—but nausea is rising in my chest like a tidal wave. I feel sweat beads cluster on my face and my breathing grows uneven. Katrina is totally oblivious.

"Well, you should know, Mommy thinks we need more security. And she also came up with a last minute brilliant idea. Everyone's going to have a jar of butterflies on their seats. After we say our vows, they're going to release them. All those butterflies flying in the air will be so Cinderella-ish."

Her words drift in one ear and out the other. I could give a flying fuck about butterflies. Right now, all I can think about is the horrific nauseous feeling that's consuming me. I break into a cold sweat and my head starts spinning like a Disneyland teacup. I'm on the verge of throwing up. I need to get to a toilet fast! Except I'm so queasy I can't take a step. I sway on my feet and clutch my stomach. And then BLECH! I wretch. Hot vomit pours out of my mouth like molten lava from a volcano and spreads like a puddle on the glistening floor. I hear Katrina shriek in disgust as I continue to puke my guts out. I puke until I can't anymore and my throat is so sore it hurts to swallow. Holding on to the edge of the liquor cabinet, I straighten. Katrina glowers at me. The expression on her face is one of utter contempt.

"I'm sorry," I mutter, my voice a mere croak.

"Dammit, Brandon. If you're coming down with something, I'm out of here. The last thing I need on my wedding day is to be sick."

She pivots on her heel and stomps to the front door. I hear it open and slam shut, and then her car peels away. Shivering and dizzy, I sag down against the liquor cabinet until I'm crouched on the floor, my pool of vomit surrounding me. I bury my head between my knees to block out the odiferous smell and to soothe my monster headache along with my unyielding heartache.

All I want is Zoey. For her to be here to take care of me and to let me hold her.

My beloved mentor's words swirl through my head. *Act with your heart. Lead your dreams and land them.*

The next to last thing *I* need on my wedding day is to be sick. Sick with regret.

The very last thing I need is Katrina.

Chapter 14

Zoey

It's been a non-stop busy day with one demanding client after another. To top it off, I've had to act cheerful when inside my heart is splintering. Tomorrow, Brandon and Katrina are getting married. And the wedding of the century is going to be televised live on TV. It's been the talk of the tabloids and the Internet as well as every news and gossip show on TV. There's been a ton of speculation about the cost—with some saying as much as ten million dollars—as well as about Katrina's dress, the celebrities attending, and Bratrina's secret honeymoon destination. The massages and soft music do little to soothe my mind or my heart.

Just as I'm about to call it a day, Madelyn, the spa's high-strung, bag of bones manager, comes bursting through the door. While Posh is known for its tranquility, she's an exposed nerve. Behind her bony back, everyone calls her Madwoman.

"Zoey, you can't leave. We have a VIP client who needs a massage. Her regular masseuse fell ill, so you have to step in. Of course, we'll pay you overtime, and the client is a very generous tipper."

With a shrug and a sigh, I say, "Fine." I was so looking forward to going home and having a hot bath—my new form of relaxing. But what's another hour. Or another dollar?

Madelyn flashes a smile. "Wonderful. I'm going to personally bring her back. Remember, she's one of our very important clients."

I set up the table, light a scented candle, and dim the lights. The soft relaxation music is still piping through the sound system.

Draping a clean sheet over the massage table, I hear Madelyn's voice. "Zoey, this is our very special client..."

I spin around. Our eyes clash. Not Madwoman's.

Rather, another mad woman far more evil...

"...Katrina Moore." Madwoman's voice drifts into my ears. "Be sure to give her extra special attention. She's getting married tomorrow to Brandon Taylor, so she wants to look and feel her very best."

Katrina smiles at me wickedly as she slips out her cell phone from the pocket of her spa robe.

"Enjoy your massage, Ms. Moore," singsongs Madelyn before sauntering off. Smirking, Katrina makes a call.

"Hi, darling."

My heart stutters. She's called Brandon.

"What are you up to?" she purrs, drumming the pink rhinestone-studded case with one of her long manicured fingers.

"That's wonderful. I'm just having a massage. And then I'm going home to get ready for our *wedding* rehearsal." Thumbing her blinding ten-carat diamond engagement ring, she puts a special emphasis on the word "wedding," flinging it at me like a dagger. "Love you too."

Another dagger. How much pain can I take?

She ends the call and smugly gives me the once over. "Well, well, well, if it isn't Miss Fatty Pants. I'm glad to see you've found yourself a new job. That hideous uniform suits you well."

Rage replaces the pain. My blood is curdling. *Nice to see you too, bitch.*

"I'll be right back," I hiss, gritting my teeth. "In the meantime, please take off your robe and lie on the table face down."

Before stepping out of the room, I heat up the oil in the warmer. I then make a quick bathroom run and return. Katrina is stretched out as instructed on the massage table. Her long, toned, bronzed body glows under the dim lights along with her lustrous platinum hair that's piled high on her head. The thought of her lying in bed with Brandon sickens me. And tomorrow they will be husband and wife.

"What's taking so long?" she snaps. "I'm ready."

I'm ready too. Oh am I. In my massages classes, they taught us beauty equals pain. I'm about to put that equation into action. The massage oil is warm. Make that very warm. As in scorching hot. Taking a washcloth, I lift the bottle into my hand and careful not to burn myself, pour a generous amount on Katrina's taut sculpted back.

Jolting, she yelps. "What the fuck are you doing?"

"What's the matter?"

"Whatever you put on me is burning my skin!"

"Oh, I'm sorry. I must have overheated the oil." *Hehehe!* "It'll cool off in no time. How do you like your massages?"

"I like them hard. The way I like my men. By the way, I asked for a hot stone massage not a deep tissue one."

"No problem." I grab a couple of stones—the largest ones—from my supply counter and pour the cooled off oil on them until they turn a lustrous black.

One in each hand, I press them against her sublime flesh, making circling motions on her upper back.

"Harder," she grunts.

She asked for it. She wants it hard. I'm going to give it to her just the way she likes it. An evil smile snakes across my lips.

I press the rocks deeper into her skin, and then as she moans with pleasure, I begin to pummel her. Harder and harder and harder. Her moans morph into shrieks.

"Oh my God!" She bolts up. "What are you doing, you bitch? You're trying to kill me!"

"You told me you like it hard."

"Fuck you, you jealous cunt! She jumps off the table and throws on her robe. "You're going to pay for this! I'm going to get your fat ass fired." Tying the belt, she storms out of the room.

I don't give a shit. I hope I've left her with a lot of ugly bruises. Maybe her wedding gown or rehearsal dress is backless. She can show them off.

I'm done for the day. If I have to pay the consequences, I will. I don't even want to be a masseuse. I have bigger dreams. I tidy up the room, and then make a discovery.

Katrina's cell phone. She's left it behind. Screw the bitch. I'm not running after her to give it to her. Let her suffer without her lifeline. I toss it into a pocket of my uniform.

One heartbeat later, my cell phone pings. I slip it out of my other pocket. It's a text from Madelyn. *Please stop by my office before you leave.*

My stomach knots. The end may be in sight.

Madelyn's office is spacious and elegantly appointed like the rest of the spa. The lighting is muted, and her uncluttered desk reflects her anal personality. She taps her spindly manicured fingers together. Her tight Botoxed face is, as usual, pinched.

"Have a seat, Zoey." Her voice is frosty.

Wordlessly, I lower myself into one of the two upholstered armchairs facing her.

"Katrina Moore told me you tried to kill her."

"Well, I wouldn't exactly call it that," I say defensively with laughter in my voice.

Madelyn purses her scarlet lips. "Whatever. Perhaps she over exaggerated, but you nonetheless gave her an unacceptable massage."

I remain silent.

"This is not the first time I've had a complaint about you. A gentleman told me you didn't give him what he wanted."

Fucking Brandon complained?

"Who might that be?" I ask, knowing damn well. Asshole!

"Sheldon Greenberg. He's a major player in this town."

The fucking pig!

As I seethe, Madwoman continues. "You know, usually I go by the three strikes and you're out rule, but, Ms. Hart, you seem to be a loose cannon. Your lack of professionalism with two of our biggest and most respected clients leaves me no choice. I can't afford to ruin our reputation. Ms. Moore has threatened to go to the tabloids and besmirch us if I don't take action. God forbid!" Icicles form in her eyes while she pauses. "You're fired."

You're fired. The two words vibrate in my ears as if served on a tuning fork. When Brandon fired me, my heart sunk into a dark abyss. I cried for days. But to my surprise, I feel an unexpected lightness of being. Almost euphoria. Fuck Madelyn. Fuck this place. Fuck all my demanding clients. Tomorrow I can sleep late.

I rise to my feet, and with a bright smile, I spit out two words: "Thank you."

On the way to my small but cozy apartment, I stop and collect my mail. The usual. Bills, bills, and more bills. I'm not sure how I'm going to pay them, now that I don't have a job, but decide to worry about that tomorrow. I'm more focused on the small padded yellow envelope with no return address. There is, however, a UPS overnight tracking number. My name and address are written in large, unrecognizable block print letters. It's marked fragile. Dropping the rest of the mail on my kitchen counter once inside my apartment, I tear open the mysterious envelope, and my breath hitches in my throat at the sight of the contents.

A DVD. The season finale of *Kurt Kussler*. The episode that screened at MIP but won't be airing until Monday. There's no note.

My emotions are in a jumble. The euphoric high I experienced after getting fired quickly gave way to gloom on my drive home. I thought about Katrina and Brandon getting married tomorrow. And now this. With a jittery hand, I set the DVD on the counter and stumble to the refrigerator. Thank goodness, I have a half bottle of Trader Joe's Two-Buck Chuck left. Since leaving Brandon, I've been drinking more than usual; the wine's helped numb my pain and sorrow.

After shakily pouring a glass, I collect the DVD and head into the living room. Sinking into the couch, I take a long sip of the cheap Chardonnay and then place the glass on the coffee table. I'm still gripping the DVD, anxiously debating whether to watch it or not. It has to be Brandon who sent it to me. But why? And how did he get my address? Maybe that bitch Madelyn gave it to him. Is he still playing a sick sadistic game with me? He wants to be in my face the night before he marries that other bitch. Pour salt into an open wound?

Fuck him! Fuck this DVD! As I'm about to break it in half with my bare hands, my cell phone rings. I fish for it in my pocket and then glance at the caller ID screen. Unknown number. Who the fuck can it be? Some stupid solicitor? I hit "answer" because I'm in the mood to rant.

"Fuck you. Never call—"

A soft, sultry voice cuts me off. "Just watch the DVD. I hope you understand."

Brandon! How the hell did he get my new number? The phone shakes in my trembling hand. My heart is thumping and tears are welling up in my eyes. Why does he still affect me? Why can't I get over him? Why can't he leave me alone and stop taunting me?

Before I can hang up on him, he whispers one more word. The magic one: "Please." The line goes dead.

Every nerve ending in my body is a sparking fuse. I take another big gulp of the white wine and stare hard at the DVD. The burning urge to destroy it slowly dissipates and is replaced by an irrational desire to watch it. Setting both the wine glass and DVD down, I retrieve my laptop from my desk. I haven't gotten around to buying a TV or DVD player yet so this is the only way I can view it. I plop back down on the couch with the computer in my lap and, with an unsteady hand, insert the DVD.

The opening credit montage immediately plays. While I've seen it countless times, my heart hammers. Brandon in all his sexy action poses takes my breath away, eliciting a Pavlovian response that makes my ovaries fall apart. After he stares into the camera pointing his big gun and says, "Get it. Got it? Good!" he fires it—*Bang!*—and the final credits appear. *Written by Brandon Taylor.* I almost forgot he wrote the finale. My breath hitches once more. It's entitled "Unforgettable."

My eyes are already watering and the episode hasn't even begun. As much as he's a sadistic bastard, I must be an even bigger masochist. A glutton for pain and punishment. I have no idea what to expect. Brandon never told me a thing about it except it was going to have a mind-blowing twist and a cliffhanger ending. Said he was sworn to secrecy.

My eyes never leave my computer screen. The episode is intense, action-packed, and suspenseful. His faithful assistant, Melanie, has been by his side for most of the show. They've found some more clues to the whereabouts of The Locust, Kurt's late wife's assassin. Weary, emotionally drained Kurt needs a break. He tells Mel he's going to go out for a coffee; she insists on fetching it for him, but he declines her offer. He just needs to get out. Clear his head. As he departs his office, Mel looks at him with a combination of lust and love in her eyes. She loves him so much! It's been so obvious over the course of the series. If only he would wake up!

I grow emotional and then my heart jolts. An ear-deafening explosion! Mel's eyes grow wide and she screams, "No!!!!!" She sprints out the door.

My heart almost stops. Kurt's on the street, lying in a dark pool of blood. He's been shot!

"Oh my God!" I hear myself gasp with Mel. A mixture of shock and sadness whips through me. This can't be happening!

Sobbing, Mel falls to her knees beside Kurt. She hastily removes her sweater and presses it against his gushing chest wound while cradling his head in her other arm. He's still conscious, but barely. His hooded eyes burn into hers.

"Mel, did anyone ever tell you you're smart... you're funny...and you're cute?"

My heart's racing; tears spilling. Oh my God. These are the very same words he told me that night in his car when he called me on my charade with Jeffrey.

Tears cascading, Melanie shakes her head and rasps, "No."

The faintest of smiles splays on Kurt's lips. "Well, I'm telling you."

"Save your strength," Mel begs.

Kurt's blood seeps through her sweater, his breathing labors, and his eyelids grow heavier. Mel panics.

"Kurt...Kurt...can you hear me? Please! Stay with me!"

Kurt's breathing grows harsh. He's fading fast. Mel leans into him.

"Don't you dare die on me, you self-centered, egotistical asshole," I hear myself sob out together with Kurt's hysterical assistant. These are *my* words. The exact ones I said to Brandon when I found him lying unconscious after his hit and run. Oh my God! Were they in his subconscious? Did he have a memory breakthrough?

"Don't give up. Please! I love you so much!" The words tumble off my quivering lips in unison with Mel's as her tears fall onto Kurt's face. I know what's coming next. She traces her hand along his strong jaw and then, her lips lower onto his. Still cradling his head in her other arm, she kisses him. Sobs clog her throat. Just like they did mine on that fateful day. I replay that moment. And relive the all-consuming, passionate kiss that I hoped would magically wake Brandon up. Like in a fairy tale.

Mel pulls away and holds Kurt in her loving, teary-eyed gaze, brushing her hand through his hair and losing all hope. Sobbing so loudly, I almost don't hear Kurt's last line:

"I love you too, baby." His eyes close and the screen fades to black. *To Be Continued.* And then the closing credits come on, rolling to a too familiar song— "Unforgettable" sung by Brandon, his voice unmistakable. My throat constricts so tightly I can barely breathe.

A tsunami of big, ugly, snotty tears pours down my face. My keyboard is covered with them. When I swipe at them, they only multiply. Sobs wrack my body. My emotions are in turmoil. An excruciating combo of passion, sorrow, and confusion floods my veins. What cruel mind game is Brandon playing with me now? What is he trying to say? My phone starts to ring.

I slam my laptop shut, and still sobbing, I hug a pillow tightly, my tears soaking the fabric. My phone keeps ringing and ringing and ringing until it dies a silent death.

Chapter 15

Brandon

Why won't she pick up her phone? I call again and again. And each time, it goes straight to her voice mail. Dammit, Zoey. Pick up your phone. I had to bribe her boss to give me the number as well as her address. The skinny bitch cost me ten thousand dollars. All that for nothing. I bet Zoey's turned her cell off.

Frustration mounting, I pace my house. I know, just know, she watched the episode. And without commercials, it ran about ninety minutes so she must be done with it. I speed-dial her one more time. Again, the call goes straight to voicemail. I can't bear to hear her voice again, so I text her, begging her to call me. Tossing my phone on the couch, I take long angry steps toward the bar and pour myself a Scotch. As I'm about to put the tumbler to my lips, the sound of my front door opening and slamming shut distracts me. Heavy footsteps get closer. Setting the tumbler on the bar, I spin around and face him. It's Scott, my manager. Crap. He's come by to drive me to the wedding rehearsal that's taking place in a half hour at The Four Seasons. He's going to be my best man. He makes a beeline for the bar and pours himself a whiskey.

My eyes drink him in. His bottle-brown hair is greased back and he's dressed in a slick, navy three-piece suit that's a little too shiny. Dangling an unlit cigarette from his mouth, he looks on edge. He downs the whiskey and gives me the once over.

"You look like shit. What happened to your face?"

While I'm no longer wearing a Band-Aid, the scab on my face is pretty nasty, and the truth is I feel sick to my stomach about the whole wedding, let alone Zoey. I tell Scott that I got into a car accident, without getting into details, and that I haven't been feeling well since it happened. I may even have the flu.

"Shit, man. Accident or not, why the hell aren't you ready? The rehearsal starts in thirty minutes, and with the Friday night traffic on Sunset, we'll be lucky if we get there in an hour."

Barefoot, I'm wearing sweats and a hoodie. I haven't even showered or shaved. "I don't have an assistant to help me." A lame excuse but true.

"What happened to the one I talked to a few days ago?"

"I fired her."

"Come on, Brandon. This is the fifth assistant you've fired this month. What was wrong with her?"

"I couldn't stand her squeaky voice and she was totally incompetent. Couldn't even bring me the right size Starbucks in the morning."

Scott rolls his eyes. "Jesus, Brandon. You're fucking impossible."

He refills his tumbler while I take a sip of my Scotch. "Do you have a minute?

"What for?"

"I need to talk to you." I haven't had a heart to heart conversation with him since I got back from Cannes. In fact, I've hardly seen him as he's been mysteriously out of town. I have no clue if he knows what went down between Katrina and me. And I've avoided talking to him about it because I don't know if I can trust him. He's a liar who could be connected to my hit and run and, to a degree, a thief as he never paid back the two grand I lent him. But what bugs me most is that he went along with Katrina and forced Zoey and Bella, the two most important and cherished people in my life, to stay away from me when I was in my coma. I've thought long and hard about firing him, but Lieutenant Mancuso, who's now working my case, has advised against that as it might arouse suspicion. Everything's so fucking complicated and I barely have the energy to deal. If only I could talk to Zoey, things might be simpler.

My manager glances down at his flashy gold watch. His eye ticks. "Okay, but make it fast. We need to get to The Four Seasons."

I head to the couch and sit while he follows me and takes his normal seat in the chair closest to me. He sets the tumbler on the coffee table and then twirls his cigarette. "Can I light up? I could really use a smoke. I've had a rough day."

So have I. I was on pins and needles, waiting for Zoey's package to arrive. When I checked the tracking number online, I knew it had and had a moment of reprieve. But she won't talk to me and I'm facing the biggest day of my life. A life-changer. Scott's nasal voice cuts into my anxious thoughts.

"So, I guess that's a yes," he says, already lighting up.

As much as I hate him smoking in my house, I don't have the wherewithal to fight him. I have bigger things on my mind.

Returning his gold lighter to his breast pocket, he puts the cigarette to his mouth. He takes a drag and blows out a cloud of smoke. "Shoot."

"I'm having second thoughts about marrying Katrina."

He practically chokes on the next puff of his cigarette. "Are you fucking out of your mind?"

In answer to his question, I may be, but I don't tell him that. "I'm still not feeling it with her."

Scott's voice rises with anger. "What the fuck do you mean?"

I'm not sure what he knows, so I play it safe. "We still have no connection, physically or emotionally."

Another puff and he flicks his ashes in the ashtray. "You had a major head injury. You suffered amnesia. Your doctors said it would take a while for your memory to return."

"Scott, it's been five months. I remember a lot of things."

"Like what?" he asks nervously, his brows shooting up.

"Just about everything."

His twitchy eye flutters and his face tenses while I continue.

"Everything except my accident and the weeks leading up to it."

He quirks a small smile and then takes another long draw of the cigarette. Tilting back his head, he blows a ribbon of smoke into the air. "That's good, Brandon. It's only a matter of time until you remember your history with Katrina."

"Maybe there's nothing to remember."

My bold, unexpected words swirl around in my head. While I process them, Scott's ruddy face turns ashen and his hand shakes as he lifts the cigarette again to his mouth. He takes another quick puff and then recovering, says with confidence, "C'mon, man. You two fucking knocked it out of the ballpark."

Okay, here goes. I take a deep breath and my gaze meets his twitchy eyes. "Scott, maybe you've never always leveled with me, but I've always leveled with you. I'm in love with someone else."

"One of your former bimbos?" Contempt creeps into his voice. He's hiding any sign of surprise well.

"No. Someone special. Someone you know."

"Jesus Christ, don't tell me it's that smart-ass ex-assistant."

I feel my blood pressure spike as I clench both my jaw and my hands. I swear if he says one more thing about Zoey's ass, I'm going to knock out his fake teeth. It takes all I have to contain my temper.

"You know what happened in Cannes?" I venture.

Scott stabs the butt of the cigarette in the ashtray and hastily puts it out. "Of course, I know. Katrina told me everything. You were out of your fucking mind."

"No. *She* was out of her fucking mind." My voice is combative.

"She told me you assaulted her."

Rage surges inside me. "You believed her?"

"I don't know, but the press would have. You're lucky she kept her big mouth shut."

"Whose fucking side are you on, Scott?"

"Yours." He pauses. "Listen, Brandon. Let *me* level with you."

My blood heats at his confrontational tone.

"*Brand*-man, you're a brand… It's in your name. Get it?"

Got it. Good. "Just get on with it."

"Katrina is perfect for you. The public adores Bratrina. They can't get enough of the two of you. They want a happily ever after."

"What if I can't deliver?"

Scott's beady eyes narrow. "It's simple. Your career is over. Trust me, I know her. She's a fucking loose cannon. She *will* go straight to the tabloids and smear your name everywhere—online, in print, and on TV. She showed me photos of what you did to her in Cannes. That gash was cringe-worthy."

"She did it to herself with a piece of glass."

"That's not what she says. And now, there are red welts along with black and blue marks all over her back. I saw them for myself."

I jolt. "What are you fucking talking about? I've NEVER touched her. You've got to believe me!"

"Brandon, it doesn't fucking matter. What matters is she's smart. She's America's It Girl. The public adores her. She'll play it so she's just a poor Cinderella—a victim of abuse, whether you assaulted her or not. When she shows the photos to TMZ and the handiwork of 'your' latest assault, everyone and their mother will despise Brandon Taylor. *Kurt Kussler* ratings will plummet; the show will get canceled, and your career will tank. Everything you've dreamed of—including one day winning an Oscar—will go down the fucking drain. And that's the best possible scenario. I wouldn't put it past her to go to the authorities and press charges. She'll put you behind bars." He pauses and our eyes clash, his dark and full of spite. "Do you understand what I'm saying? Are you getting the picture yet?"

My stomach in knots, I nod silently. He's just reiterated Blake Burns's sentiments but made them a far more ugly and impending reality. Yes, everything's on the line. The psychopath is holding a knife to my heart. Fucking, fucking Katrina.

My manager flashes a smarmy smile. "Good. Now, look at the bright side. You can always divorce her. You know, for irreconcilable differences."

"She'd be open to that?"

"Totally. She's even told me herself."

My mind spins. "I need to get a pre-nup by tomorrow."

Scott chortles. "C'mon, Brandon. Get real. No lawyer can do that."

He's right. I absorb his words and do the math. If we divorce, she'll be entitled to half of my fortune. But truthfully, five hundred million dollars may be a small price to pay for happiness. And true love. Zoey's adorable face flashes into my head. She's worth every penny. If only she'll take me back. There's no guarantee. Scott once again cuts into my thoughts.

"I personally know one of the top divorce lawyers

in town. He handled Katy Perry and Russell Brand's divorce among others. He can make yours happen as fast…even faster."

"How fast?"

Scott snaps his nicotine-stained fingers. "Like that."

"Send me his name."

Scott grins. "Will do. Now, get ready for the rehearsal."

"Listen, Scott. I'm not feeling good. I'm not going to the rehearsal."

Scott's eye tic starts up again. "I'm not leaving without you."

I shrug. "Then you can miss it too."

"What is wrong with you? Don't you get it?"

"I just don't feel good. Tell Katrina I'm still sick. She'll appreciate it."

Scott draws in a sharp breath through his nose and exhales. "Fine. But you sure as hell better be there tomorrow. Even if you're on your deathbed. There's a lot riding on this wedding. And not just your future."

"Don't sweat it. I'll be there."

"Good." With a look of relief, he stands up. "I'll text you that lawyer's name when I get to The Four Seasons."

Don't bother. After he disappears, I take a deep determined breath. A lot can change between a dress rehearsal and the actual shoot. Including the script.

Chapter 16

Zoey

I'm a total zombie. I didn't sleep a wink. With tears soaking my pillow, I replayed the season finale of *Kurt Kussler* in my head over and over again. With my eidetic memory, I virtually know every word by heart but still can't make sense of it. Lying on the couch with a blanket and still in my PJs, I watch it again on my laptop, and another avalanche of tears falls from my eyes as it comes to its heart-ripping conclusion. Sobs wrack my body. Why am I such a glutton for pain? In a few hours, the man I love with all my heart, body, and soul will be married to another. America's It Girl. And everyone in the world will be watching them say their forever vows. Everyone except one. Me. There's a reason why I still don't have a TV.

Drained by my tears and aching heart, I close my stinging eyes. I don't know how long I've napped when the familiar ping of my cell phone wakes me up. Groggily, I stand up, wrapping the blanket around me, and try to remember where I left it. It's in the kitchen. Please God, don't let it be him. I stagger into the adjacent room and indeed my phone is on the counter. Except it's dead. Another ping sounds in my ear. Huh? And then I remember, I have Katrina's iPhone. Identical to mine, it's in my bedroom. Probably still stashed in the pocket of my masseuse uniform.

I bet the bitch is leaving me a nasty message to return her phone. Or maybe it's mad Madelyn threatening me. I'll return it when I'm good and ready. Maybe never. In my sullen state, I derive a little pleasure thinking about how much time and effort it will take Katrina to purchase and set up a new phone. And how she must be seething and lost without it on her wedding day. Haha! No selfies for her.

The phone pings yet again as I step into my bedroom. My ugly uniform is strewn on the floor. Mental note: burn it. Another ping. Another possibility of who it could be stabs me. Brandon! My imagination runs wild thinking that he's sending her hugs and kisses. Or texting her about all the naughty things he's going to do her on their wedding night. Bile rushes to my throat at the thought of them fucking their brains out. Screw the bitch. I'm going to turn off her phone. I bend down to retrieve it, and as I hold it in my hand ready to press the off button, yet another ping sounds. Curiosity gets the better of me. Running my forefinger across the screen, I click on her text messages. To my surprise, they're not from the bitch, Madelyn, or Brandon but rather all from that sleazeball Scott. One after another.

Why the fuck can't I reach u?

On way to hotel. Call me! Urgent!

Postpone honeymoon. Need the money FAST!

Call me ASAP. I've got a big problem.

What's Scott's problem? Perplexed but intrigued, I scroll down further to a text he sent Katrina last night while I was crying my heart out over the *Kurt Kussler* finale.

Great news. He already wants a divorce. The money will be ours in no time.

My blood pounding, I process the last message. Brandon wants to divorce Katrina? He hasn't even married her. And both she and Scott are after his money? Burning with curiosity and my heart racing, I scroll through Katrina's older messages. After many exchanges with her mother about wedding details, another exchange with Scott captures my attention. It's dated Sunday, April 12, the night she showed up in Cannes.

Katrina: *I got rid of the fat bitch. LOL. I found his phone and fired her.*

Scott: *Nice work.* :)

What!? Katrina fired me? Hacked into Brandon's e-mail account and pretended to be him?

My fingertip sizzling with rage, I scroll back further. The lazy psycho bitch never erases her texts. After a few exchanges about the terms of her reality show deal—the greedy bitch wants $50,000 per episode!—my eyes grow as wide as saucers. My already rapidly beating heart accelerates.

Katrina: *Come over for a quickie.*

Scott: *A little whipping?*

Katrina: *I'm going to give it to you hard.*

Scott: *I'm hard already.*

I gasp. Oh my God! Scott and Katrina are having a sordid affair?

Frantically, I continue to scroll, my fingertip flicking the screen past a bunch of gobbledygook until another round of texts brings me to a sharp halt. They're dated March 22, three days after my encounter with Scott and Donatelli at The Farmer's Market.

Scott: *Some asshole detective may question you. Be careful.*

Katrina: *Don't worry. He questioned me ages ago.*

My mind races. Scott must have been smart enough to delete all his texts with Katrina from his phone so my father wouldn't see them. For sure, Pops would have issued a warrant for both his cell phone and computer to check for evidence. It's standard operational procedure. He confiscated and checked Katrina's phone as well but early on in his investigation of Brandon's hit and run. I recall him telling me he didn't find anything suspicious.

Yes, there were numerous phone calls between her and Scott, but they couldn't be construed as incriminating evidence since Scott is her manager and they likely talk all the time. My eyes stay focused on Scott's last two words: *Be careful*. The detective in me wonders what they mean. With baited breath, I scroll back further and then this:

Katrina: *The fat bitch is getting in the way.*

Scott: *We need to get rid of her.*

Rage whips through my bloodstream, then my heart thuds with trepidation. Scott's words whirl around in my head like a tornado. Could they have possibly intended to kill me? After scrolling through more disgruntled texts about Katrina's reality show contract, I come to yet another set that makes my eyes flutter and my heart practically jump out of my chest.

Katrina: *Worried. His memory is coming back. What if he remembers I hit him?*

Scott: *Relax. I have it covered. He won't be able to prove a thing.*

I gasp out loud. The phone shakes in my hand. My skin bristles. I can't believe what I've just read. *Hit*…as in hit and run? It has to be. Katrina ran over Brandon!! She wanted to kill him? And now, she's marrying him to get his money? And then run off with Scott?

Oh my God! It's 5:30 pm. In just a half hour, they'll be saying their vows live on TV. Panic pulses through me. Without wasting a second, I call Pops. Thank goodness, I know his cell phone number by heart. His phone rings and rings and rings. Shit. Since I'm using Katrina's phone, he won't know it's me. Pick up! Pick up! My thudding heart's in my throat. Come on, Pops! Please pick up! After the fifth ring, he does. Breathlessly, I tell him everything. The words fly out of my mouth. He listens intently and then says:

"Get dressed, Babycakes. We have a wedding to crash."

Chapter 17

Brandon

It's a fucking spectacle. A circus. Hordes of fans and paparazzi surround us as our Cinderella-inspired horse and carriage heads down Doheny en route to The Four Seasons. Katrina, dressed in her hundred thousand dollar gown that takes up most of the carriage, smiles brightly and waves to the crowd as if she's royalty. Gucci, dressed in some frou-frou pink concoction, is on her lap and cocks his head at me, confounded. Butterflies swarm my stomach. I'm nervous as shit. The biggest moment of my life awaits me. I don't know if I can pull it off. But, at least, I'm wearing my lucky cufflinks. The gold monogrammed ones that belonged to my father. As I fiddle with them, the memory of Zoey trying to put them on the night of the Golden Globes flashes into my head. Her incompetence was so adorable! When I look back, I loved her even then. The fond memory sparks a small smile, but it falls off my face as soon as we pull up to the entrance of the imposing hotel. My anxiety returns full force and crashes through me like an avalanche.

Shouts of "Bratrina" echo in my ears. The pumpkin-like carriage comes to a halt and, after we're helped out of it, we're whisked away by security. As we're led to our holding quarters, I glimpse the sprawling garden where our ceremony is taking place. Hundreds and hundreds of guests are being escorted to their seats, and a production crew is running around attending to last minute details.

The holding quarters are no less frenetic. Hair and makeup people are scuttling about the spacious, elegantly appointed suite, putting finishing touches on the bridesmaids and groomsmen, all hired from Central Casting. Katrina's mother Enid, dressed in a peach gown, is shouting into a walkie-talkie.

"Where the hell is the last groomsman?" Her brows furrow as much as Botox will allow them. "What!? I don't care if he's got pneumonia. Call Central Casting, you moron, and get someone over here NOW!"

She catches sight of us and her face brightens.

"Mommy!" exclaims Katrina, running over to hug her. "My special day is here at last!"

"Darling, you look absolutely divine. Monique's dress is perfection."

"I hope Daddy will see it on TV. It's such a shame

they wouldn't let him out of prison for my special day."

Enid rolls her eyes. "There's a reason your father is behind bars. For all I care, he can rot in his cell."

"Whatever. Talking about cells, I think I left my phone at the rehearsal last night. Did anyone turn it in?"

"No, darling, I'm sorry."

Enid's attention is thwarted. Another x-ray thin, chicly dressed woman with a tight black chignon and skin so taut it may crack joins them. After giving Katrina the once over, she fluffs out her poufy white gown. She must be the designer, Monique Hervé. She gives Enid a flirtatious wink before addressing her client.

"Katrina, my love, I want you and Brandon to take a photo with the *In Style* photographer. A picture's worth a million bucks."

Before I can blink, I'm posing with Bridezilla.

"I'd like to get a shot of the two of you kissing," says the young female photographer who has us huddled side by side on an elegant loveseat. Gucci is on Katrina's lap. With the width of her gown, there's barely any space for me.

Katrina makes a face. "Absolutely not! I don't want to mess up my lipstick, and besides, I'm the only one who belongs on the cover. A close-up."

To my great relief, Katrina gets up, leaving me with The Gooch, and poses for the photographer. Blowing kisses. Swirling around in her voluminous gown.

Flinging back her platinum locks that are held back by a diamond tiara and a mile-long tulle veil that trails along the carpet. While she continues to prance around the suite, the production staff mikes me up.

"We're going to need some cutaways and sound bites," says a jeans-clad AD from Katrina's reality series as she hides a mike under the lapel of my tailcoat. A scraggly cameraman aims a handheld camera at me. I vaguely remember seeing him before in my hospital room when I woke up from my coma.

"Fine," I mumble, responding to the AD.

"Just answer my questions, but make sure you re-peat what I say. For example, if I ask you how do you feel…you respond by saying I feel blah, blah, blah, blah. And be sure to look into the camera."

I nod. "Got it."

"Great," she says with a smile and then gets right into it. "Brandon, how do you feel about marrying America's It Girl?"

"I feel both excited and nervous. This wedding is going to be unforgettable."

"Are you marrying the girl of your dreams?"

I twitch a half smile. "I'm marrying the girl of my dreams."

Before she can ask another question, Enid shouts into a megaphone. "Listen up, people. The procession is about to start. When I give you your marching orders, file out the door. Be sure to smile." Her eyes dash around the expansive room and land on Scott.

My manager, the best man, is in a far corner, pacing and talking on his cell phone. His face pinched, he seems to be spewing some angry words at whoever is on the other end. A lit cigarette dangles from his other hand.

"Scott, put the phone away and get rid of that awful cigarette," chides Enid. "You're first. Let's move it."

Slipping the phone into the breast pocket of his tux, my manager takes one more inhale of his cigarette before tossing the butt to the floor and stamping it out. His left eye is twitching and a deep frown line is etched across his forehead. He seems on edge. Passing by me without as much as saying a word, he heads out the French doors to the garden. Blowing an air kiss to Enid, Monique, the maid of honor, follows him outside.

Enid does a headcount of the groomsmen, who all look like Ken dolls. Seething, she lifts her walkie-talkie to her pursed lips. "Where the hell is that replacement? What do you mean he's stuck in traffic? You're fired!" She hurls the handset across the room. "Screw it."

"Groomsmen, move it!" she shouts out with a loud snap of her bony fingers. "Let's go. Chop chop!"

My stomach tenses as I watch them file out the door.

The dozen blond, busty Barbie-lookalike bridesmaids are next. Followed by two professional children who have been hired to be the flower girl and ring bearer. Then it's my turn. I can't get my feet to move. It's like they're stuck in cement.

"Jesus, Brandon. Move it already!" Enid yells.

Katrina fires me a scathing look. "What the hell are you waiting for?"

Taking a deep breath, I finally get up and amble toward the exit. Here goes nothing.

I take slow, hesitant steps down the flower-lined aisle as a harpist with an angelic voice performs "A Dream is a Wish Your Heart Makes" from Disney's *Cinderella*. Inside, my heart is beating a hundred miles an hour. I call upon all the acting skills I have to act the part of the excited groom. My eyes dart left and right to meet the celebrity-filled crowd—a glittering blend of men in black tie and women in dazzling gowns and jewels. The Hollywood elite. There's only one special person I'm searching for. My wishful heart's only dream. She's nowhere in sight. I do, however, spot the cast and crew of *Kurt Kussler* among the gazillion guests as well as Blake Burns and his wife Jennifer. They meet my gaze, and by the concern written on their faces, I know they sense my anxiety. Two cameramen flank me as I head up to the canopied altar, capturing my movements and expressions for the live televised event. The walk to the altar seems like an eternity. I just want this day to be over.

I join a very anxious Scott, beaming Monique, the plastic bridesmaids and groomsmen, the bickering children, and the craggy preacher, who looks to be an out-of-work actor in need of rehab, under an extravagant gazebo draped in tulle and a multitude of exotic white flowers. Several photographers and cameramen surround us, including one who is operating an overhead camera. As the orchestra starts playing "The Wedding March," I turn to watch my Cinderella-bride stroll down the aisle arm in arm with her mother. In her free hand, she holds an extravagant bouquet along with a leash that's attached to Gucci. The poor little dog seems freaked out. My bride, however, is enjoying every glorious minute and mugging for the cameras that follow her march down the aisle. I wonder if the real Cinderella—my beloved Zoey—is watching. That night after our James Bond marathon, she promised she'd be here, but I have no hope she'll show. Why should she? My already rapid heartbeat speeds up as Katrina reaches the altar. While her mother steps to the side, she sidles up next to me. We turn to face the preacher. The scent of alcohol on his breath is so thick I can taste it.

"We are gathered here today…" His slurred words go in one ear and out the other. My brain is focused on only one thing. I've got to do it. I've got to! Every nerve in my body is buzzing with anxiety. Every muscle clenched. Before I know it, it's vow time.

"Do you, Brandon Taylor, take Katrina Moore to be your lawful wedded wife, for richer or poorer, in sickness and um…*hiccup*…in health until death do you part?" Gucci growls at the drunken preacher. *Sic him!*

I can feel Katrina's eyes on me. In fact, the whole world's eyes are on me. I draw in a sharp breath, and on the exhale, I ready myself to face Katrina and respond. My heart is hammering like a jackrabbit's. I hesitate.

Katrina grows impatient and hisses, "Brandon, just answer his question. For God's sake, how hard is it to say 'yes'?"

One little word is on the tip of my tongue, but before I can get my lips to move, a familiar gruff voice sounds in my ears.

"Katrina Moore…"

I spin around. My eyes almost pop out of their sockets. And my heart practically stops.

Marching down the aisle are Pete and Zoey. My true princess! Pete is holding up his badge.

Zoey, looking totally ravishing in a body-hugging, ivory chiffon dress and matching stilettos, stays behind while her father steps up to the altar. Our eyes connect, sparks flying. My dormant cock is finally up for the wedding of the century.

"What the hell is going on?" yells Katrina.

Pete jumps in. "Don't move. You're under arrest for the attempted murder of Brandon Taylor."

What!? My heart skips a beat as Katrina's jaw crashes to the floor. Gucci sees Zoey and breaks free. Wagging his tail, he scampers down the aisle and runs circles around her.

Enid rushes to her daughter's side and shrieks at Pete. "What on earth are you talking about, you lowlife scumbag?"

With a poker face, Pete slips his hand into a pocket of his trench coat.

"Ms. Moore, does this look familiar to you?" In the palm of Pete's hand is the green Venetian glass heart he showed me months ago.

Katrina's eyes widen. "That's my lucky heart I bought in Venice when I was at George Clooney's wedding!"

"Well, it's not your lucky heart today."

Katrina's flaring eyes latch on to Zoey. "I bet that little whore stole it from me!"

Pete remains cool, calm, and collected. "Actually, we found it at the scene of Brandon Taylor's hit and run accident. Which puts you there."

Katrina huffs. "Bullshit. I was with my mother." She turns to Enid. "Right, Mommy? Tell him."

A shaken Enid opens her mouth, but before she can get a word out, Pete shuts her up.

"Perhaps, Ms. Moore, this will refresh your memory." He reaches inside his other coat pocket and holds up a phone. I recognize the pink rhinestone-studded case instantly. It's Katrina's! The one with all the incriminating photos taken in Cannes that she never lets out of her sight.

Katrina gapes. "My phone! That fat bitch stole that

too!"

I shoot a glance at Zoey. With a smug little smile, she shrugs her shoulders. God, I so love her!

Pete persists. "Perhaps, these texts will jog your memory." Zoey's father reads aloud an exchange between her and Scott. Holy fuck! I can't believe my ears. Fucking Katrina ran me over! Then left me for dead at the scene of the accident! And Scott covered for her!

Katrina gasps. In shock, my eyes flit from Katrina to Scott and then to Zoey. While the color on Katrina and Scott's faces completely drains, the smile on Zoey's adorable face widens. Low grumbles sound among our attendees, who aren't privy to what's going on. The inebriated preacher, also oblivious, sways on his feet.

It's Scott's turn to say something. The color on his face goes from chalk-white to fire engine red. His twitchy eyes narrow with fury at Katrina. "You stupid idiot! You didn't erase the texts?"

Katrina's lips quiver, but before she can get out a sound or word, Pete fastens a pair of shiny handcuffs on her wrists as he reads her rights. Hushed gasps fill the air. The preacher hiccups again and then passes out. I swear, I don't know if I'm in the middle of a soap opera, horror show, crime drama, sitcom, or a really sick reality show.

Katrina's reaction doesn't help me figure things out.

A mixture of terror and rage flickers in her venomous eyes. "Take these off me, you pig!" She tries desperately to pull the handcuffs apart.

"Let's go," orders Pete, grabbing her elbow.

"Let go of me!" cries Katrina, frantically trying to break loose of his forceful grip. "Mommy, call our attorney!" Desperation fills her voice. And then she turns to Scott. I follow her gaze.

"Do something, you asshole!" she screams at my manager.

A deafening boom sounds in my ear. All at once, Katrina, her mother, and the crowd of spectators shriek. Scott's mouth opens wide and a loud, pained groan escapes. Clutching his stomach, he crumples to the floor. Unconscious, he's sprawled in an expanding puddle of blood. Holy fucking shit! He's been shot!

A thunderous voice rises above the frantic crowd.

"No one move. Or I shoot her!"

I flip around and my eyes grow wide again. Oh my God! Scott's assailant is gripping Zoey by her neck and wielding his gun. I recognize his ugly pockmarked face immediately. It matches the police artist's sketch of Zoey's mother's murderer! The motherfucker who also killed my parents. Frank Donatelli!

Releasing Katrina, Pete faces him squarely and pulls out his gun from his holster. "Put your weapon down."

Donatelli snarls. "Fuck you, bastard."

To my absolute horror, he puts his gun to Zoey's head. Terror flashes in her eyes. Paling, she bites down on her trembling lip while Gucci, at her feet, barks non-stop at her captor.

"If you don't put *your* gun down, I'm going to blow her brains out."

For the first time, fear washes over Pete's face. "Please don't hurt her."

"Did you hear me? Drop your fucking gun."

Slowly, Pete lowers his gun to the ground.

Walking backward with Zoey in his grip and his gun glued to her head, Donatelli stumbles down the aisle. His eyes stay on Pete. My eyes stay on Zoey. The wedding spectators stay glued to their seats, afraid of being shot by the madman. Even the photographers and cameramen are paralyzed with fear. Rage blasts through me like a Molotov cocktail. The Kurt Kussler in me is exploding with the burning urge to go after them, but I hold myself back. Gucci, however, doesn't waste a moment and chases after his beloved Zoey. *Go, boy!*

"Fuck," mumbles Pete under his breath. But the second they disappear from view, he squats down, retrieves his gun, and springs into action.

"I'm going after them." He dashes down the aisle at breakneck speed, and I'm right behind him, my coattails flying. Maybe Kurt Kussler couldn't save his wife, but I'm going to save my future one. There's no fucking way I'm going to lose her.

Two breathless minutes later we're in hot pursuit of Frank Donatelli. Pete's siren blares in my ears. My eyes stay on Donatelli's red Ferrari as Pete expertly maneuvers his beat up Impala through the traffic on Doheny. He talks into his communication device.

"I need backup," he says after telling the dispatcher about fallen Scott. "The suspect is traveling south on Doheny. He's armed and dangerous and has a hostage." He pauses. "My daughter."

My thudding heart is in my throat. While I've done a lot of action-packed chase scenes as Kurt Kussler, nothing compares to this real-life version. The camera crew actually wanted to follow us, but Pete demanded they stay behind.

Donatelli hangs a sharp left on Venice. I hang onto my seat as Pete follows him and races down the busy boulevard.

"Fuck!" Pete grumbles. "He's heading toward the freeway."

Traffic comes to a standstill as we zigzag down the thoroughfare and run every red light. I'm blown away by the speed and precision of this old Chevy.

"Have you ever fired a gun?" Pete asks me, without taking his eyes off his target.

While I've actually never fired one with real bullets, my character Kurt Kussler is a natural with a gun. I tell him I have.

"Open the glove box. There's one inside."

I snap it open and reach for the weapon. It's a Chrome Magnum 45...exactly the gun Kurt Kussler carries. It feels good in my hand. There's a difference between a big flaccid dick and a big hard one. The loaded gun feels like the latter. Adrenaline pumps through my veins. I'm ready for action.

"I'm going to take a shot," I tell Pete.

"You know what you're doing? The bastard's got my daughter."

"And my future wife."

"Go for it!"

Chapter 18

Zoey

Terror fills every crevice of my being, but I try hard not to show it. It's almost impossible for me to believe I've been dealt this unbelievable fate. The very man who killed my mother is going to kill me.

"Shut that fucking dog up!" Donatelli screams at me.

Gucci is on my lap. He followed us out of the hotel and then jumped into the car before we peeled away. He hasn't stopped barking.

I caress his furry head. "Shh, Gucci. Be a good little boy." To my relief, he calms down, but my fear intensifies.

"If that mutt opens his fucking mouth one more time, I'm going to silence him." He points the big gun he's still holding in his right hand at us as he deftly maneuvers the speeding car with his left.

I shiver. A siren sounds in the near distance.

Donatelli glances into the rearview mirror and scowls. "Goddamn fucking cop!"

Pops!! Knowing he's in hot pursuit instills me with the tiniest bit of courage. I clutch Gucci as Donatelli makes a sharp, screeching turn off Venice and heads down La Cienega. He weaves in and out of the insane traffic, ramming cars and knocking others into one another. Any way I look at it, my life's about to be over.

"Are you going to kill me the way you killed my mother?"

For a brief second, Frank takes his eyes off the road and glares at me. "What the fuck are you talking about?"

I stare at him squarely. Terror gives way to rage. "You killed my mother! I saw you on the pier."

"What the hell?"

My voice grows tearful and louder by an octave. "How could you forget? Twenty years ago! The Santa Monica Pier. You shot my mother! And the man next to her. And then you tried to shoot me!" The painful memory fills my head. Mama slumped over the railing, bleeding to death. And then swirling, helplessly, hopelessly in the angry sea as the Nat King Cole song plays. It's all so unforgettable.

"You took my mother from me!" I cry out.

Donatelli blinks hard and then scrunches his ugly

face. "Jesus fucking Christ. You're that fucking little girl? The little bitch who's given me nightmares my whole life?"

I bite down on my quivering lip to stifle my sobs, but can't stop the onslaught of tears. "I've never forgotten you either, you bastard!"

"Shut up! Or you're next!"

That does it. I can no longer hold back. Sobbing, I begin to pound him.

"You fucker!"

"What the fuck are you doing?" The car swerves and horns blast from every direction.

I pound harder and more furiously. Gucci barks madly.

"Say goodbye, you fucking cunt."

He turns to face me again and aims his gun at my head. The trigger clicks.

The sound of a gunshot roars through my ears.

Chapter 19

Brandon

Bingo! Thank my father's lucky cufflinks. And thank you, Kurt Kussler.

On my first shot, I nail the motherfucker's tire—just the way Kurt did to The Locust's car in one of this season's episodes. I fire my Magnum at the other back tire as his smoking car skids off the street and crashes into a deserted storefront.

Zoey leaps out of the car. *Run, Zoey, run!* But before she gets far, the bastard tackles her. He yanks her to her feet again, holding her hostage with his gun to her head.

My heart is beating a gazillion miles a minute as Pete steps on the gas and then comes to a screeching halt. In unison, we jump out of the car.

"Give it up, Donatelli!" yells Pete, aiming his gun.

"Fuck you!" In the blink of an eye, the fucking

bastard does the unthinkable. He fires his gun. The explosive bang echoes in my ears.

"Pops!" screams out Zoey.

Fuck. Pete is down. It's just me now. In the near distance, sirens roar.

"Put the gun down," the fucker yells at me.

"Let her go first."

"Maybe you don't understand English. Drop the fucking gun."

He presses the barrel of his gun against Zoey's temple. Her desperate eyes meet mine. I have no choice. I let the gun fall from my hand.

"Let go of her now!" I say authoritatively.

He snickers. "Are you out of your fucking mind? I'm going to take your car and her with me. One move and she's dog meat."

Fuck. He played me. I think hard about scooping up the Magnum, but think twice. He'll either shoot Zoey or shoot me. Or take us both out.

The tension in the air is as thick as fog. My eyes don't blink as the bastard takes his first step toward Pete's vehicle, gripping a terrified Zoey by her neck. A loud growl sounds in my ear. My attention is diverted. It's Gucci! Flying out the window of Donatelli's smoking car, he makes a beeline for the bastard. Go, Superdog!

"Ow!" yelps Donatelli as Gucci attacks him, biting his ankle like a rabid pit-bull. The dog's relentless.

Growling, his razor-sharp teeth stay locked on him even as the gun-wielding bastard attempts to kick him off. Go, Gucci! I fucking love this ten thousand dollar mutt.

"Get this fucking dog off me!"

As a cursing Donatelli tries to fend off Gucci, Zoey breaks loose.

"Run, Zoey, run!" I shout out as I hastily scoop up my gun.

Zoey takes off like the wind, but Donatelli pivots toward her and aims his weapon. He fires. He misses. Zoey trips in her heels. Shit! He's about to take another shot.

Holding my Magnum steady in both hands, I aim it at him and pull the trigger back.

"You motherfucker!"

He turns and I fire. *Boom!* The deafening gunshot reverberates in my head as I watch the motherfucker go down. *Holy shit! I got him!* I'm a fucking real life action hero. Sliding the gun under the waistband of my tux pants, I lunge over to Zoey, who's sprawled on the ground.

"You okay, baby?" I ask as I scoop her up into my arms. Sobbing, she clutches me the way a child does a parent, folding her arms around my neck and her legs around my hips. Her head presses against my pounding heart. Nodding, she whispers my name through her tears.

"Oh, Brandon." Her words are like prayer. I tenderly brush my hand through her silky hair.

"It's over now, Zo. The bastard's dead. I nailed him right between the eyes."

"No, it's not, you cocksucker." A familiar rasp captures my attention. Shit! It's Donatelli, staggering to his feet, dripping with blood, his gun in his hand. Zoey screams.

"Don't look, baby!" With Zoey burying her face against my chest, I yank out my Magnum and aim it at the bastard. One of us is going to die, but it's not going to be me or my baby.

"You fucker," croaks Donatelli, fumbling for the trigger.

"No, *you* fucker." I fire once and hit him in the chest. "That's for killing her mother." I fire again, getting him in the gut. "That's for killing my parents." I fire a third time, hitting him smack in the balls. "That's for taking my girl...and *this* is for calling me a cocksucker." I shoot him one final time in the nut sack for good measure. My lips snarl. "Get it. Got it? Good."

The gun falls out his hand as he collapses back onto the ground. Lying in a pool of blood, he's dead for sure. My focus stays on the bullet hole between his wide open eyes. Bastard! Fucking bastard! I hope he can still see me from the fiery depths of hell.

Tossing my weapon, I tenderly kiss the top of Zoey's scalp. "Baby, it's really over now."

She slowly lifts her head and her misty eyes meet

mine. "What about Pops?"

"Yeah. What about me, Babycakes?"

Zoey gasps. Her tears of grief give way to tears of joy. "Pops! You're okay!"

A little disheveled, Pete staggers our way. He kisses Zoey on the cheek and then meets my gaze. "Tell Kurt Kussler that he should always wear a bullet-proof vest."

He rips open his trench coat to reveal his. It's a little shredded. I laugh. "I will. He'll appreciate the tip."

A warm smile spreads on his face. "Thank you for saving my little girl."

I feel myself blushing. It feels totally amazing to be a real life action hero.

A big grin flashes on Zoey's face as she casts her eyes down. "He was wearing his lucky cufflinks."

Lucky indeed. On my next heartbeat, Zoey's delicious lips are on mine. I deepen the kiss with my tongue, cherishing the taste of her. The scent of her. The feel of her. And every bit of her in my arms.

Gucci's barking breaks us apart. While a beaming Pete excuses himself to join the myriad of cops who have arrived on the scene, Gucci's persistent barking grows louder. Zoey ruffles my hair and laughs. "I think he's jealous."

"The Gooch is going to have to learn to live with the two of us."

Zoey holds me in her twinkling big brown eyes. "Brandon Taylor, what exactly do you mean?"

"Well, with Katrina likely going to serve some prison time, this little rascal's all mine now. I hope you're okay with that."

"Mr. Taylor, what else are you trying to tell me?"

"There's a wedding in progress at The Four Seasons. If I recall, you promised you'd be there for me."

"I'm sorry. Does showing up a little late count?"

"No excuses. Would you like to attend the rest of it with me?"

Her eyes grow wide as my words sink in. I can feel her heart rapidly beating against mine. Her kissable mouth drops open. There's no need to tell her that I was never going to say yes to Katrina. After my confrontation with Scott last night, I decided to spurn her on national TV. The consequences didn't matter to me. What mattered was marrying the right girl. Like my wise, beautiful mentor Bella said: To act with my heart...and land my dream. A stammer cuts into my thoughts.

"B-Brandon, are you asking me to marry you?"

"Yeah. That's what I'm trying to do. Well...?"

"Is this how Kurt's going to propose to Mel?"

I roll my eyes; she's killing me. "I don't know. I haven't written the episode yet."

She laughs. "I think it would work out perfectly."

"Is that a yes?"

She cradles my head in her hands. Another passionate, all-consuming kiss is the only answer I need.

Chapter 20

Zoey

Brandon borrows Pops's car. I must say I totally enjoy seeing Mr. Lamborghini behind the wheel of his beat up Chevy. The truth is Brandon looks good in any car. I can't take my eyes off him as today's insane events whirl around in my head. Brandon once said he'd kill for me and he did. At last Donatelli is dead. It's hard to believe. And it's even harder to believe we're getting married. I should pinch myself, but if this is a dream, I never want it to end.

"Brandon, can we make a stop in Beverly Hills before we head over to The Four Seasons?"

He turns to look at me and his violet eyes burn a hole right through me. A dazzling smile curls on his lips. "Only if we make it quick. Hold on."

On my next breath, we're racing up Doheny toward Wilshire Boulevard, the police siren blasting.

I've always put down Pop's old Chevy, but now know it has its benefits.

My real life action hero is in seventh heaven. "Man, this is more fun than being Kurt Kussler. Do you think your father will let me borrow his car after we're married? It's the bomb!"

"Maybe," I say. "Everything's negotiable." I wink at him. "And who knows, it could be a wedding present."

My husband-to-be shoots me a hopeful, loving look.

"Well hello, dear. So nice to see you again," says Beatrice. To my shock and relief, the Tiffany saleswoman who I met several months ago is still here. Her voice is a little frosty. I don't blame her. I never came back for the ring. She must think I'm just a looker. Or a bullshitter.

"Let me know if there's anything I can help you with."

I glance down at the display case and my heart sinks. While there are dozens of dazzling diamond rings inside it, the magnificent amethyst and diamond ring I coveted is not among them.

The pencil-thin saleswoman starts locking up the cases. "Just so you know, we'll be closing in fifteen minutes."

My muscles tense. I don't have much time.

Beatrice's throaty voice drifts into my ears. "Did you come back for your ring?"

"Yes," I say glumly. "My fiancé's back in town and I wanted to show it to him."

"Oh. Is he here?" A thick layer of doubt colors her tone.

I nod. "Yes. He'll be here any minute. He's just parking the car."

I study the other rings, hoping to find one that'll call out my name. Not one does.

Beatrice's gasp diverts my attention. I gaze up at her shocked face. Her mouth is agape. Finally, her lips move.

"Good heavens!"

A nuzzle on the back of my neck sends me spinning. Brandon!

He smacks a kiss on my lips and then says, "I valeted the car. The valet is taking care of Gucci."

I smile and then turn to face Beatrice, who's still in a state of shock.

"This is my fiancé," I say brightly.

She clasps a bony hand to her still wide-open mouth. "Oh my God, *you're* marrying Brandon Taylor?"

"Yup."

"In just a few minutes," chimes in Brandon with a Cheshire grin. He straightens the spaghetti straps of my ivory dress, the one Chaz gave me for my birthday. Little did I know it would be my wedding gown. Nor did I ever think my birthday wish would come true.

"Wait right here," Beatrice says eagerly. Her demeanor and tone have totally changed. My eyes stay on her as she scurries to the back of the store.

"Do you like any of these?" asks Brandon, gazing down at the display case. "You can have anyone you want."

I sigh. "You know what. I don't need a ring. I just need you."

He draws me into his arms. His hardness pressing against my abdomen only magnifies the feelings this incredible man has for me. His piercing violet eyes claim mine.

"The same, baby. Let's just pick out some wedding bands and head over to The Four Seasons."

He tilts up my chin with a thumb and his lips crash onto my mine. Our tongues twirl and swirl in another passionate embrace. I can't get enough of him. And I still can't believe this fairy tale has come true.

"I have something you may like." Beatrice's voice breaks us away. Flushed, I meet her gaze. Her steel-gray eyes are twinkling. She sets a small Tiffany-blue box on the glass counter and slowly takes off the lid.

I clap my hand to my mouth and gasp. Oh my God! It's my ring! The breathtaking amethyst and diamond one I fell in love with! The ring whose stone reminded me of Brandon's violet eyes and fit me perfectly.

Beatrice smiles at me warmly. "It's a one of a kind so I kept it in our safe. I had a hunch you might come back for it one day."

With tears in my eyes, I hug her. "I don't know how to thank you."

"I do," says Brandon, enjoying my emotional fireworks. "Let's do this right."

My misty eyes never stray from him as he removes the ring from the box and gets down on one knee. He clasps my left hand.

"I love you, Zoey Hart, with all my heart, from here to the moon and back. Marry me."

The entire staff of Tiffany's has gathered around us, but I'm almost oblivious. Rivulets of tears stream down my cheeks as the man I will cherish forever slips the magnificent ring onto my ring finger. My heart is exploding with love, and my body is overflowing with joy. I hear Mama. She's here somewhere, watching over me. Singing "Moon River." Her beautiful nightingale voice fills my head while two beautiful violet eyes fill my sight.

"Yes! Yes! A thousand times yes!"

Oohs, aahs, and applause break out all around us. Another all-consuming scorching kiss drowns out the crowd.

Oh, Brandon Taylor. My dream maker…Wherever you're going, I'm going your way.

Chapter 21

Brandon

When we return to The Four Seasons, the place is swarming with news crews, reporters, and cops. I have no clue if the production team from Katrina's show is still here, but for sure, our guests have abandoned the hotel. Well, all except Blake Burns and his wife Jennifer, who are mingling with the Conquest Broadcasting news crew. I quickly find out from one of the officers that Scott's still alive and has been transported to Cedars. In the corner of my eye, I see Katrina's mother Enid talking to one of the reporters. She catches sight of me as well as Zoey, who's holding Gucci (minus the tutu) by his leash. Leaving the reporter hanging, she stomps up to me.

"Where the hell have you been?"

I contain my laughter. "I've been busy saving lives."

Steam blows out of her nostrils. I can virtually see it. "The only life you should be saving is my daughter's. She's been arrested!"

"She deserves to be." In the car ride over here, Zoey filled me in on everything she discovered on Katrina's cell phone. The fucking psycho bitch. Not only did she run me over, but she also was after my money and screwing around with Scott—something I always suspected. There are still a lot of missing pieces and unanswered questions, including motives and Scott's relationship with Donatelli. But I'm sure they'll unfold in the weeks to come.

Enid's taut face scrunches as much as it can. "The bail is set at one hundred thousand dollars. You need to take care of it immediately!"

I've had enough of Enid and Katrina spending my money.

Rage flickers in Enid's unblinking eyes. "What the hell are you waiting for? Chop chop!"

And I've had it with all her chop chops.

"I'm afraid I can't."

Enid grows hysterical, her voice shrill. "What do you mean? You're her fiancé. You're supposed to be marrying her!"

I stare at her squarely. "Enid, I had no intention of marrying Katrina."

"What?" says Zoey before Enid can.

I take her into my arms and kiss the top of her head.

"Baby, it was always going to be you."

Zoey gazes up at me with puppy eyes that make me melt.

Enid's face turns as dark as her heart. "What the hell to you mean?"

"I mean I was *never* in love with her. Meet my new fiancée."

"Hi," squeaks Zoey.

Enid glares at her, aghast, and then flares her eyes at me. "What! You're ditching my daughter for this chubby p-peon?"

A growl sounds in my ear and the next thing I hear is a loud shriek from Enid. She gazes down and shrieks again.

"Fucking dog! Somebody help me! Get this monster off me!"

Zoey is laughing; so am I. Gucci has attacked Enid. Bitten her twice in the ankle. Zoey scoops him up in her arms before he does it again.

She tuts. "Bad doggie."

Good doggie! We exchange an amused look as Enid limps off, mentioning something about a lawsuit and shouting for someone to give her first-aid. She needs a whole lot more than a Band-Aid to fix the hole in her warped mind.

Setting Gucci back down, Zoey takes in the frenetic scene. A little overwhelmed, she knits her brows. "Brandon, maybe we should have eloped."

I flip up her chin with a thumb. "Nah. We're going to do it right here and the whole world is going to watch. Maybe not on Katrina's reality series, but at least on tonight's news. By the time we say, "I do," it'll be all over YouTube, Instagram, and TMZ.

"Really?"

"Really." She's so fucking adorable she's giving me a hard-on. If you ask me, no better way to get to married. And the sooner we get married the better. It's a good thing my custom-made tux pants have extra crotch room.

Catching sight of me, hordes of reporters rush up to me. I'm bombarded with blinding flash bulbs and burning questions. To most of them, I respond: "No comment."

A young Latino reporter from Conquest Broadcasting breaks out of the pack and shoves her mike in my face.

"So, Brandon, will you still be getting married tonight?"

Smiling, I squeeze Zoey's hand. "That's the plan."

"To Katrina Moore?"

"A change of plans. Meet my new fiancée, Zoey Hart."

A gazillion flashes go off. Zoey smiles brightly for the cameras and waves. Meet America's *newest* "It Girl."

Before any reporter can besiege her, I say, "We just

need to find someone who can marry us." The drunken preacher from Central Casting is long gone; he must work by the hour and be at the bar.

The reporter's face lights up. "I can do that. I'm a newly ordained minister from the Universal Church of Life."

The Church of Life. No other ministry better suits Zoey and me. Let's get this show rolling. Lights! Camera! Action!

Five minutes later, we're standing in the flowered gazebo under the starry sky. Gucci is with us, Zoey still holding him by his leash. Blake and Jen have agreed to be our impromptu best man and maid of honor. And miraculously, Pete and his wife Jo have gotten here just in the nick of time along with Zoey's brother Jeffrey and his fiancé Chaz. Myriad camera crews and reporters surround us. Facing my soon-to-be wife, I slide a platinum band on her ring finger until it lines up perfectly with her amethyst ring and recite my vows. They're almost identical to those I exchanged with my late wife Alisha on *Kurt Kussler.* But the words mean something so much deeper now. I'm not acting the lines. I'm saying them for real. They come from the bottom of my heart.

"Zoey Hart, from this day on…You. Are. Mine. I promise to cherish you and protect you for as long as I live. For richer or for poorer, in sickness and in health, in good times and bad times until death do us part."

With her free hand, Zoey slips a matching band on my ring finger. Her chocolate eyes are glistening with tears. She repeats some of my words and then adds a few of her own. "Brandon, my love, I will be yours for all of eternity. You'll always own my heart even after I part."

The words of our officiant pronouncing us man and wife drift into my ears as I take my beautiful wife into my arms and kiss her madly. She moans into my mouth. Amidst the clicking cameras, I can hear Auntie Jo sniffling.

"Mr. Taylor, what's our next activity?" Zoey asks softly after we finally break the kiss.

I trace her luscious lips with a finger. "Mrs. Taylor, one you'll never have to use your imagination for again." *Nor will I.*

A short fifteen minutes later, we're steps away from the sunken tub in the non-cancelable penthouse suite the bitch put on my credit card, about to finish what we started in Cannes. And start so much more.

Chapter 22

Zoey

The crazy events of today are a swirling blur. I still can't believe I just married the man every woman on the planet wishes she could have. The man of my dreams. There's happy. And there's beyond happy. I'm in the latter category. The luckiest girl in the world.

My lips stay latched on Brandon's as he carries me into the penthouse suite of The Four Seasons. Tightening my grip around his strong shoulders, I open my eyes a sliver to take in my surroundings. Wow! It's like a palace in the sky. All sleek shiny marble, muted silks and velvets, and touches of gilt. With elegant furnishings that include a baby grand piano complete with a bucket of champagne and wraparound windows offering a spectacular panoramic view of sparkling LA.

He transports me down a long hallway until we reach a palatial bedroom. An enormous four-poster bed with a mile-high duvet and a mountain of fluffy pillows dominates the room. On the opposite wall, a built-in fireplace casts a warm glow from the fire inside. On the mantle and every surface, scented candles burn and mingle with the intoxicating scent of fresh flowers.

He sets me down on my feet by the bed and then captures my lips with another passionate kiss. I melt into him.

"I wanted to finish what we started in Cannes, but I can't wait," he breathes into my mouth. Planting his lush lips back on mine, he undoes the back zipper of my dress and then slides the spaghetti straps off my arms. Chaz's creamy chiffon creation puddles at my feet, allowing me to step out of it. I'm left with just my ivory lace undergarments and my heels. Cupping my shoulders, Brandon stares at me reverently and then kisses me everywhere he can.

"Oh, Zoey, you're so fucking beautiful and tonight you're finally all mine. All I want to do is make endless love to you."

"Oh, Brandon! The same! I've missed you so much."

"You have no idea how much I've missed you. Help me undress."

On my next heated breath, I undo his bowtie and the buttons of his shirt while he unfastens his lucky cufflinks and puts them securely in a pocket of his tux pants. I smile at the memory of dressing him in his tux on the night of the Golden Globes and broaden the dreamy smile as I stand now before him and help him out of his formal wear. Feverishly, I unclasp his trousers and zip down his fly, freeing his enormous cock. In a few swift moves, he kicks off his shoes and steps out of the pants while I toss his jacket and shirt to the floor. As he unhooks my bra and removes it, I soak in his beautiful body. He's the epitome of manly perfection with his taut flesh, pronounced muscles, and defined contours. The glow of the fire and candlelight makes him even more sublime. Surreal. A sex god. My god. I run my fingers along his strong jawline just to make sure he's real. He gropes my breasts in his soft hands and bends to kiss them. A low rumble sounds in his throat as my body responds with a rush of hot tingles. Reality sets in. There's nothing that stands between the two of us except a veil of love.

"I can't wait another minute, my beautiful wife."

My breath hitches. He called me his wife. I have to get used to this new four-letter word. *Wife.* The word's beauty resonates in my ears.

Lifting me back in his arms, he sets me down on the massive bed and then crawls onto it. His magnificent cock is erect and ready. His smoldering eyes stay riveted on me and then he bends over, his mouth blazing a trail of kisses from my quivering lips to my inner thighs. My pussy is flooding like a river and need pours from my core like a waterfall. I moan from the exquisite pleasure he's giving me.

"Zoey, listen to me," he says, sliding off my lace thong and then my shoes.

My senses heightened, I'm all ears. All nerves. All desire.

"You're completely mine now."

I have to adjust to the fact that I'm no longer just Brandon Taylor's assistant. I'm his wife. He's my husband. My lover. My real life action hero. My prince. My life. The man who said he'd kill for me and he did. I'm overflowing with love for him. I need for him to possess every part of my body.

"Brandon, please make love to me."

His mouth makes its way back up my legs. He nuzzles my inner thighs.

"I'm going to do a lot of things to you tonight."

"Like what?" I breathe out, already so aroused.

"Things I need to do," he whispers against my scorching flesh. "Things I think you want me to do." He draws in a deep, lustful breath. "Zoey, I want you to submit to me. Let me love *all* of you the only way I can."

My beating heart is about to ricochet out of my chest. I so want him to own me. Possess me. Take total control. Haven't I always been his sub? At his command?

"Brandon, I'm your wife. Own me. Please own me." My core's on fire, every cell ignited. I'm begging as sinfully as I can.

His violet eyes are smoldering. "My beautiful wife, by the end of tonight, I will own every inch of you." He clasps my hand and reverently kisses my amethyst ring. "You are my life. I want you to trust me. Can you do that?"

Speechless, I nod as he continues.

"I'm going to pleasure your body and not stop until I've memorized every crevice, every curve, and every sexy imperfection. You're going to lose count of how many times I make you come."

I hold my breath in anticipation. While one of his hands stays splayed on my inner thigh, the other slides over my slick mound. At the touch, I flinch. Using all his fingers, he kneads it, his thumb giving extra special attention to my humming clit. Moans that start off soft grow louder with each one that spills from my lips.

"Oh, baby, you're so fucking wet for me." His voice is deep and low and so sexy.

I whimper as he picks up his pace. The rotations come at me harder and faster. My clit ablaze, he's taking me to the edge. I'm so ready to combust.

And then a new unexpected sensation assaults me. Still grazing my inner thigh, he plunges a long finger into my pussy. Shoving it in as far as it'll go. He begins to pump it vigorously while his other hand indulges in my clitoral massage. His finger keeps hitting that mega-sensitive spot, bringing me closer and closer to the precipice. The building pressure inside me goes from intense to unbearable as my body prepares for the inevitable.

"I'm going to come!" I scream out.

"Not yet, baby. I'm going to fuck you into oblivion. The only thing you'll remember is me coming inside you as I make you come over and over again."

On the next beat of my heart, he spreads my legs farther apart and throws my feet over his shoulders, the weight and heat of his body lingering over me. He leans in and wedges his spectacular cock inside me with a helping hand. I let out a loud groan as his fullness fills me. It sails smoothly into my sea of wetness.

"Jesus, baby. You feel so fucking good. I've missed this so much." Setting his hand on the bed parallel to the other, he hits my womb and then slowly pulls out. Another few long, steady strokes and then he begins to hammer me madly, taking me to the hilt with every passionate thrust. Each time he hits my magic spot and rubs his length against my clit, the friction creates a new barrage of sparks between my melting legs. His harsh breaths fill my ears and mingle with mine. My eyes stay on his impassioned face, glistening with sweat. I cling to his tight ass, and my pussy clenches around his formidable girth as I undulate my hips to meet his thrusts. He pumps harder, faster. My whimpers morph into sobs as my body races to the finish line. A spiritual swirl of emotion and sensation overtakes me.

The sheer bliss of our bodies together is almost too much to bear.

"Oh, Brandon! I love you! I love you! I love you!" I cry out, the uncontrollable words not coming from my throat but some place so much deeper inside me. My eyelids lower as if my whole body is saying a prayer.

"Keep your eyes open, baby," Brandon pants out. "I want you to watch me. And see what you do to me when I make you come with me. And never forget how much I love you."

I know better than to disobey him. My gaze stays on him as we both soar toward orgasms of unworldly proportions. The intense expression on his face is one of pure determination and tortured ecstasy. Passion shoots out of his half-mast eyes.

"I want you to roar my name so loud the bell captain hears it," he pants out.

I nod feverishly, unable to say a word. I'm so, so close to coming. So near euphoria.

"Now, baby!" On the next forceful thrust, he lets out a loud feral grunt. At the savage sound, I fall apart. My orgasm travels inside me like the forked fault line of an earthquake. I roar out his name as I shudder with rapture around his juddering length. His volcanic release bathes me.

My legs still wrapped around his neck, he buries his face against my belly.

"Oh, baby, that was fucking incredible. And we've

just begun. The night's still young."

We fuck our brains out till the wee hours of the morning. By the time we blissfully fall asleep in each other's arms, we've made love in the tub, on the floor and the kitchen counter as well as on top of the baby grand. He's fucked me from the front and from behind and I've blown him to pieces.

Tonight was just the beginning. The world is ours and we have forever.

He's mine.

I'm his.

We're one.

And nothing can come between us.

Chapter 23

Zoey

Like gemstones, they dance around me. Topaz, sapphire, coral, and amethyst too. Fish of all colors, sizes, and shapes. I breathe in and out of my regulator, and behind my mask, my eyes grow wide with awe. Like my life, this is all surreal. I'm on Day 3 of my month-long honeymoon with Brandon Taylor. The man of my dreams. I don't know how he did it, but he's mapped out a total James Bond honeymoon that includes all the destinations featured in *Casino Royale*. The Bahamas is our first stop where we've been lodging at the five-star Ocean Club in Nassau (complete with a rented Aston Martin and a dog sitter for The Gooch.) At the end of the week, we'll move on to Europe and culminate our trip in Venice. I'm so sore I'm seriously not sure if I'll be able to do any sightseeing. Though sightseeing is not high on Brandon's list of priorities.

The mild, salty Atlantic is soothing. A welcome relief. Floating in the crystal clear turquoise water, I experience an incredible lightness of being and freedom like none other. It's like I'm weightless and flying. Just six months ago I suffered from an immeasurable fear of the ocean, but Brandon changed all that by teaching me how to swim. To think I would have missed out on all this other worldly beauty and wonderment makes my skin prickle beneath my wetsuit.

In the otherwise magical silence of the sea, only the soft, melodic sound of bubbles blowing fills my ears while a rush of love fills my heart as Brandon holds my hand and points to a moray eel that slithers out from behind a coral reef. The florescent green creature emits a glow, but it's nothing compared to my own electrical glow. As the shimmering snake-like fish wiggles by us, Brandon repositions me so I'm perpendicular to him, my fin-covered feet almost hitting the ocean floor. With one arm wrapped around me, he removes his regulator and then removes mine. His lips descend on my mine, and breathing into his mouth, I lose myself to him. All oxygen leaves my lungs. There's a lot Brandon says he can teach me to do under the sea. My husband. My lover. My master.

We break from the kiss and return our regulators to our mouths. And my eyes grow round again. My tranquil heart practically beats out of my wetsuit.

Unable to contain my astonishment, I point with my finger, urging Brandon to turn around and see what I'm seeing. First a dolphin. And then Mama! She's a beautiful mermaid, her vibrant red hair spread out like a sea fan as she swims my way. And Papa is alongside her holding her hand. I break away from Brandon and propel myself forward as fast as I can to meet them. Mama is just as I remember her, maybe even more beautiful with her flawless shell-white skin and sparkling emerald eyes. And the man with her so handsome I can see why he is her forever love. There's an ethereal quality to both of them. Angels of the sea. They take me in their arms for what feels like an eternity.

"Oh, Mama! Papa! I've missed you so much!" I say silently.

"We've never left you," I hear Mama say, her eyes glimmering with happiness.

"You're so beautiful, my little girl," says Papa just like he did when I was a toddler.

I'm overwhelmed with emotion. "Mama, Papa, I want you to meet someone." I turn to face Brandon as he swims my way and then I turn back around to face my beloved parents. My eyes dart in all directions and then my heart sinks to the ocean bottom. They're gone! Brandon entwines his fingers with mine and with his other hand signals upward. He wants us to complete our dive. I'm under his command.

Spiraling upward like two helixes, we shoot out of the water. We both remove our regulators and lift our masks atop our heads.

"Brandon! Did you see them?" I ask breathlessly, treading water.

"The pair of paparazzi?"

"That's not funny!"

"The pair of barracuda?"

"No. Mama and Papa!" Frustration underscores my voice.

My gorgeous husband, his face glistening with flecks of the sea, flicks the tip of my nose and laughs. "My beauty, you must have been hallucinating. That can happen when you're under the water for a long time."

"No! I wasn't hallucinating! They were there! You have to believe me!"

His twinkling violet eyes dance with amusement. "You're so fucking adorable. C'mon, let's chill." Before I can say another word, he silences me with another fierce kiss that takes my breath away.

Five minutes later, we're lying down, bared to each other, on the V-shaped forty-foot hull of the sleek cigarette boat we've rented. My head rests on Brandon's rock-hard pecs and I can hear his heart drumming in my ears. Half-drunk mojitos are by our sides. The hot tropical afternoon sun beats down and warms us. He traces lazy, ticklish circles around my toasting nipples.

While tingles travel downward to my inner thigh area, my mind is still focused on my underwater encounter. I saw Mama and Papa. I know I did.

Brandon breaks into my thoughts. "Baby, what did you think about your first dive?"

"It was amazing." It really was, but I know I can't convince Brandon that my parents were there. I go for another angle. "My love, do you believe in life after death?"

He twists his head toward me. "I don't know. With all that's happened to me, I try to live in the moment and make memories. What about you?"

"Yes. I do."

"Really? So, what are you going to come back as?"

"A tall, blond, slender siren."

He grabs a fistful of my wet hair and gives it a tug. "Don't. You. Dare."

His deep, dominant voice is almost a threat. I jolt. Not from fear but from an unexpected sensation. A glacial sting hits me. An ice cube! Brandon's removed a large one from his mojito glass and placed it on my nipple. The bud hardens like a bullet at the frigid sensation while the tingles between my legs intensify. I can feel the cube melt against my heated skin, the cold liquid seeping down my cleavage and trickling onto my chest. Between my legs, another hot liquid accumulates. I'm so fucking turned on I want to jump out of my skin.

On my next breath, he rolls on top of me, the cube

still so cold and big between us. His weight pins me under him and his piercing violet eyes hold me hostage. He anchors himself on the palms of his hands and raises his head. His mouth goes down on my nipple, his warm tongue lapping the cold water from the melting cube and replacing the numbness with his wet heat. Lifting one hand, he takes the cube and rubs it around my other nipple while he continues to suck its partner. The sharp contrast sends another rush of arousal to my core, like the tide coming in. A loud "aah" escapes my throat.

"Baby, don't ever change. I love you just the way you are."

He makes me smile. With a fiendish glint in his eyes, he maneuvers himself so he's able to pry my legs apart with a single thrust of his powerful knees. A cool hand crawls between my thighs and I moan with pleasure as he caresses my slick cleft.

"Mrs. Taylor, promise me you'll never become anyone else. This is the only pussy I want."

"Mmm," I sigh as his thumb circles my engorging clit.

"I need to hear words." Without warning, he trails the ice cube down my abdomen, causing me to arch beneath him from the shock of the cold. A shiver skitters down my spine and then I gasp when the cube presses against my throbbing clit. My pelvis tilts up as much as it can beneath him. I'm in a state so heightened and helpless it's borderline unbearable.

"I promise I'll always be me…your go-to Zo," I spit out, so eager for more of the exquisite pleasure he holds in his hands like a bag of magic tricks.

"*My* fuckable go-to girl." A wicked but satisfied smile lights up his face. His eyes burn into me like the glorious sun as he resumes stroking my numbed clit with his thumb. And then another trick. And another cube. This one lodged deep in my pussy. I scream with shock. The fire inside me instantly starts melting it.

"You're dripping wet for me," he growls, applying more pressure and making me squirm beneath him.

The truth is I've been wet for him 24/7, both in the sea and on land. And I think he's had a permanent hard-on. The two of us haven't been able to get enough of one another. We've been inseparable and insatiable. But what he's doing to me now is incredible.

"I'm going to take you, Mrs. Taylor. I'm going to fuck you so hard you're going to scare the fish when you come."

"Oh Brandon," I moan, cupping his strong, stubble-lined jaw. My clit is lit up like a bundle of dynamite, ready to detonate. "Please!" I beg, quickly remembering my magic word.

On my next heated breath, his enormous erection thrusts inside me, consuming me inch by magnificent inch. The heat of his swelling cock is a shocking but delicious contrast to the ice cube. I'm shivering and melting at the same time.

"Oh, baby, you feel so fucking good," he groans as he drives into me, pressing the cold cube against my womb.

"Shut up and fuck me," I plead, on the brink of pain and pleasure.

"You're going to get it."

In one swift move, he does something unexpected. He rolls onto his back, taking me with him so I'm on top, his cock still deep inside me. My muscles clench around it like a fist.

"Fuck. That feels so good, my princess."

I love when he calls me princess. And I love being on top. Somehow, it's always deeper and more empowering, the orgasm so intense I see stars.

He begins to pound me ruthlessly, so hard the boat rocks. My ass lifts into the air with each forceful thrust. He grips my hips while I hold onto his shoulders as if he's a life raft. I can feel the ice cube shrinking and cold water trickling down my inner thighs as he bangs into me. A tidal wave of an orgasm unfolds inside me. I'm ready to burst and scream.

"Oh Brandon, I can't hold on," I cry out. "I'm going to come."

"Not yet, baby. Stay with me. You can do it."

Is he out of his fucking mind? Yes, he is!

On the next powerful thrust, he pulsates inside me and then I hear another magic word. "Now. Come for me, Zoey. You're all mine."

I explode. He explodes. A cacophony of grunts and screams. It all happens at once. The ice cube all but vaporizes with the molten liquids we share. I collapse onto Brandon's chest. Our chests rise and fall in harmony, slowing with each breath. So content, beautiful Brandon runs his hand through my damp hair and hums an unforgettable melody.

I cling to him like the song of love he is. Yes, that's who he is. Unforgettable in every way. And that's how he'll stay.

My heart swells with pure joy. Mama's words swirl around in my head. *We never left you.* A truth so powerful it almost hurts.

"Oh, Brandon, tell me you'll never leave me!" Tears well in my eyes.

"Never, baby. You'll always be mine."

My heart is bursting at the seams with those I love. My Brandon. Mama and Papa. Pops, Auntie Jo, Jeffrey, and Chaz. And our little Gooch.

They will live in my heart forever. That's what makes them unforgettable.

Epilogue

Zoey

One year later

My wedding changed my life. Not only did I become Mrs. Brandon Taylor, but I also became an instant celebrity. An overnight media star. The world's newest "It Girl." The newscasts of our wedding went through the roof and the photo of us kissing after we exchanged our vows was splashed all over the Internet and on the cover of every gossip magazine around the world. I have to say that some of the headlines weren't flattering. Like *More Beats Moore…Chubster Scores Kussler…*and *Chubby Lands Royal Hubby.* But I didn't really mind. And to my amusement, we were instantly dubbed *Branzo.* Hey, it could have been a lot worse. Like *Branzoey,* which to my ear sounded like some kind of Italian fish or pasta.

Or that machine that re-surfaces the ice in the middle of a hockey game. Brandon agreed. In fact, he loved it. It reminded him of his idol, Marlon Brando.

For women around the world, I was more than a celebrity; I was their idol. An overweight Plain Jane who landed Prince Charming—*People Magazine's* "Sexiest Man Alive." America's newest "Sweethart" as the press playfully called me. Worshippers started fan pages on Facebook and tweeted me left and right. I personally responded to every email, Facebook message, and tweet. I wanted my fans to know that dreams could come true. I'd wished for Brandon to marry me on my twenty-fifth birthday and soon after he did.

So much happened after we got back from our whirlwind honeymoon. Pops sucked the shit out of Katrina. Holding hands, Brandon and I watched him in action behind a one-way mirror. Demanding a lawyer, she refused to answer his questions as he wore her down. Her big shot attorney attempted to come to the rescue—along with Mommy—just before Pops showed them the texts she'd sent to Scott. Katrina paled while her attorney cringed. Enid passed out.

Claiming innocence—it was just an accident, yeah right!—Katrina balked when her attorney told her she could be tried for second-degree murder and put away for twenty-five years. A deal was struck for a hit and run felony charge, putting her in a penitentiary for five years. Parole at three, if she behaved. Katrina sobbed. I almost felt sorry for her. But Brandon told me to spare my tears. The psycho bitch deserved what was coming to her.

Someone else should have been put behind bars too. Scott Turner, Brandon's manager. Or should I say former manager. He survived Donatelli's gunshot though he has to wear a colostomy bag for the rest of his life. My husband felt bad for him, but I felt he strongly deserved it. A fitting reminder. The asshole needed to see the shit he was.

While convalescing in the hospital, he confessed everything in an attempt to get off scot-free, no pun intended. He and Katrina were just fuck buddies in every sense of the word and never intended to get married. It was all his idea to hook up Katrina with Brandon. He introduced them at the Chateau Marmont and threw out the idea of a stunt marriage to further both of their careers. Brandon thought Scott was out of his mind. What he didn't know was that both his manager and Katrina were after his money. The plan was that right after they married, Katrina would divorce him and get half his fortune—five hundred million dollars, of which Scott would get thirty percent—one hundred fifty million dollars. They both desperately needed the money—Katrina to support her extravagant lifestyle now that both her parents were broke and Scott to pay off exorbitant gambling debts to the Mob.

Katrina furthermore thought the stunt marriage would revive her sagging career. The ratings for her reality show, *America's It Girl,* had plummeted and the series was about to be canceled. A live televised wedding to Brandon Taylor, *People Magazine's* "Sexiest Man Alive," could definitely save it and make her a mega-star and the darling of the media. So marrying and divorcing Brandon could bring her both fame and fortune.

The plan sounded perfect—but there was one problem. Brandon, who went on several well-publicized dates with Katrina, discovered he couldn't stomach her. She was a stuck-up, self-centered bitch. He didn't want to go along with it. But this didn't stop desperate Scott or Katrina. Katrina stalked Brandon and tried to cajole him, and with the help of Scott, informed the paparazzi and reporters about their encounters so photos of them together would appear everywhere along with articles about their "heated" romance. She even went as far as kissing Brandon in public against his will, which made the front page of many tabloids. Brandon was furious, but Scott advised him to ignore it. In fact, denying the relationship might have reverse consequences and convince the public it was true—that he and Katrina were an item. Sadly, that's how Hollywood works.

But fed-up Brandon wasn't deterred. On the day Katrina's show was up for renewal, he threatened to call a press conference and set the record straight about his relationship with the reality star once and for all. Plain and simple, there was none. Terrified this revelation would end both her show and her career, Katrina drove up to Brandon's house to try to convince him to not to talk to the press. At least not yet. She encountered him while he was jogging down the road to his house She jumped out of her car and confronted him. He refused to give in. The bitch refused to take no for an answer and went as far as physically attacking him; he warded her off. (That's how she probably lost the Venetian glass charm). Incensed, she got back into her Mercedes, and after she started it up, she hit Brandon.

This is where things get murky. Knocking Brandon to the ground unconscious, Katrina freaked out. She called Scott in a panic for advice. She was insistent it was an accident. That in her agitated state, she'd accidentally put the car in reverse rather than in drive and hence had rammed into Brandon who was standing behind it. When Pops asked Scott if he thought Katrina had deliberately run down Brandon, he honestly didn't know. Though he did say it was a possibility—the girl was insane. And with that thought in the back of his mind, he told Katrina to leave the scene of the accident. The last thing they needed was a murder rap. So, Katrina, who had no conscience and used her mother as an alibi, left Brandon bleeding on the street to die. And he would have if I had not discovered him.

There's a saying—some people fall up. That's exactly what happened to Katrina and Scott. They used Brandon's coma to their advantage. After Scott forced me out of the picture by sending me to that remote Joshua Tree spa, "poor grieving" drama queen Katrina sat by Brandon's bedside 24/7 and fed the hungry press her tears and fears of losing the love of her life. Her fiancé. Cunningly, Scott used Brandon's Tiffany's credit card to purchase her ten-carat diamond ring just before he was admitted to the hospital and then spun a story that they'd gotten engaged the night before Brandon's horrific hit and run accident at his Hollywood Hills home over a romantic candlelit dinner. In addition to inviting the press to the hospital suite for exclusive interviews by Brandon's deathbed, Scott encouraged Katrina to film segments of her reality series at the hospital. Overnight, Katrina went from being the girl everyone loved to hate to America's sweetheart. And her ratings began to skyrocket.

The doctors didn't think Brandon would make it, and if he did, he might be permanently impaired with significant brain damage as he'd suffered severe head trauma from his skull fracture. Scott and Katrina played right into this. Taking a chance, they believed they could convince Brandon and his doctors that he had lost his memory if he awoke from his coma. Sure enough he did—with a real full-blown case of amnesia. Much to the luck of both Scott and Katrina. How perfect! Since

Brandon couldn't remember a thing, it was easy to convince him that he was engaged to Katrina and had agreed to marry her in a live televised event. While he was in his coma, the two of them even forged his signature on sappy Hallmark cards and mushy love letters like the one Katrina shared on *The Letterman Show* to prove he loved her. The only thing they didn't anticipate was that Brandon would start remembering things and start questioning his feelings toward Katrina. That he had none for her. His heart belonged to someone else. Yours truly.

When Pops shared this backstory over dinner with Brandon and me, we were totally blown away. It was so sick and twisted. Even the most brilliant writer couldn't come up with a plot line so unpredictably complex and dramatic. I wouldn't be surprised if some big shot movie producer optioned the rights. It made me angry. It made Brandon angry too. But it also made him sad. Scott had discovered him and been his longtime manager. His trustworthy manager *and* friend, so he had thought. Scott should have come forward with his gambling addiction. Brandon would have gotten him help and lent him as much money as he needed to get him off the hook.

"Why did Donatelli shoot him?" asked Brandon. Despite recovering his memory, he still had no recollection of the accident except for subconsciously remembering me coming to his rescue. His doctors told him he might never. It's probably a blessing. Some things are better forgotten.

"Simple," said Pops. "He missed his final deadline to make a payment to his loan shark. The Mob doesn't tolerate excuses. A promise is sacred. Don't deliver and die."

The same fate must have awaited Conrad Kremins, the sleazy, in-debt sex shop operator who was shot along with Mama. Poor Mama just happened to be at the wrong place at the right time. The same with Brandon's parents who met their untimely demise when Donatelli blew through a red light and rammed into their car.

After confessing everything, Scott escaped jail time. But after further investigation, Pops discovered that over the years, he'd scammed Brandon out of over five million dollars. Brandon didn't give a shit about the money, but the trust he'd put into his longtime manager, who'd discovered him, ate a big hole in his heart. I told him to press charges. Embezzlement could result in a minimum of three years behind bars. But Brandon didn't want to. He felt the colostomy bag and the fact that the scumbag would never work in this town again was a big enough price to pay. Though not totally on board with Brandon's lenient decision, I told him he needed to move on and find a new manager. Through Blake Burns, he did. Someone who worked fervently and honestly for many of Conquest's stars.

I almost thought Blake would recommend me. Except he had other, bigger plans in store for me. Soon after Brandon and I came back from our honeymoon, he invited me for lunch at the Conquest executive dining room. Without Brandon. At his wife Jennifer's urging, he wanted to know if I had any ideas for a TV show starring me. I was after all a celebrity now.

My heart leapt into my throat. I did! During our honeymoon, an idea had popped into my head. I hadn't even shared it with Brandon because I was still fleshing it out and I thought he might think it absurd. It was called *Perfect 10*.

"Tell me about it," coaxed Blake over our cold poached salmon.

After taking a deep breath, the words spewed out. "It's about this overweight career girl named Cindy who pines for her boss and longs to be a Size 6. Little does she know her gorgeous boss thinks she's a perfect Size 10."

"I fucking love it!" exclaimed Blake.

My blood raced through my veins. "And there's one other element. Her grandmother, a former top model whom she adores, is always telling her to lose weight and putting her on wacky diets. I envision her played by Bo Derek."

"Fuck. I love it even more. Ms. Ten herself."

There was one other major character—an overweight co-worker who had a crush on my heroine and was her best friend and confidant. I envisioned the part being played by Fat Albert, and if the show ever happened, I vowed to fight for him to co-star in it.

Five minutes later, I had a development deal. And six months later, I was on the air with my dream cast. The number one sitcom on all of television. My acting lessons had paid off. And all my dreams had come true.

I'm no longer a Size 8 nor will I likely ever be one again. Swallowing Brandon's cum on a daily basis has not been slimming. However, it's my cocktail of choice. Besides my husband loves me just the way I am. And he's made me love myself with all my flaws. When it comes to my career, I'm my own person, but when it comes to the bedroom, I belong completely to him.

Wet kisses awaken me. I pry my eyes open and smile. It's little Gucci, on my chest, wagging his tail, his big brown eyes in my face.

"Good morning, baby boy!" The pillow next to mine is vacant. "Where's Daddy?"

On cue, a sultry voice filters into my ears.

My gorgeous husband…holding a tray with a silver-lidded domed platter and a vase of fragrant flowers. Gucci scampers off the bed as I sit up. A pair of glistening violet eyes meets mine.

"Happy Anniversary, baby!"

A big smile spreads across my face. I wish him the same. It's hard to believe we've been married for a year. So much has happened in the last twelve months. And there are a lot more life-changing surprises in store.

Wearing sexy drawstring pajamas that hang low on his hips and bare-chested, he crawls onto the bed and sets down the tray.

"Breakfast in bed?" I purr, tracing his curved lips and admiring his pecs. I never get tired of looking at the sexy beast I married.

Placing the flowers on a nightstand, he smiles deviously. "You could say that."

"What is it?"

With a tilt of his chin, he says, "Remove the lid."

My heart beating fast with anticipation, I do as bid. Beneath the silver dome is a purple satin pouch.

"Breakfast? Should I assume there's an egg inside?"

"Well, to be honest, that's what I was going to get you for breakfast. But I ran into Blake's grandma and she highly recommended I get this instead."

Over the past year, Brandon and Blake have grown very close. And I've become dear friends with his wife Jennifer, who was largely responsible for my new career. They've invited us over to Blake's parents' house for Shabbat dinner several times, and I've had the pleasure to meet Grandma and her adorable husband

Luigi. To my shock and delight, she's the crazy octogenarian I met at the Pleasure Chest when I went there to pick up Brandon's secretive purchases. She recognized me immediately, and wouldn't you know it, the first thing out of her mouth, even before I got to light the Shabbat candles, was: *"Bubala,* so did you get the vibrator I recommended?" While Brandon burst into laughter, mortification raced through me. Needless to say, lighting the Shabbat candles with my shaking hands wasn't easy. At least Brandon and I can both laugh about that night now, and we've grown accustomed to outspoken Grandma (who has her own talk show on Jennifer's women's erotica channel) and her outrageous sexy shmexy quips.

I meet my husband's tantalizing gaze. "So what did she recommend?"

"Look for yourself."

I loosen the string of the pouch and reach inside. The contents feel like some form of jewelry. A necklace? My eyes grow wide as I remove it. It's a thick ten-inch long platinum chain with two diamond and amethyst-studded clasps at the end.

I hold it up and admire it. "Oh, Brandon. It's beautiful! Help me put it around my neck."

He chuckles. "Baby, you can wear it as a necklace tonight at dinner. I had it custom-made. It's very versatile. But right now you're going to wear this unique piece of jewelry a different way."

His hand slides under the front opening of my sheer baby doll and he tweaks my nipples until they're hard peaks. His violet eyes darken with lust.

"Are you ready, baby?"

"Oh yeah," I moan, still not sure what he has in mind.

A devilish smile curls on his lips. "Good. It's play-time."

He takes the necklace from me, and in a few heated breaths, the jeweled clasps are pinching my erect nipples. I wince with delicious pain as his nimble fingers move straight to my pussy. Two fingers plunge inside me while his thumb rubs my clit. I curse under my breath. The erogenous sensation of the extreme pain and pleasure makes me want to burst out of my skin.

"Oh, baby, you're so hot and juicy. I'm going to feast on *my* breakfast."

"Oh yes, baby. Please do!"

After a sharp parting of my legs, Brandon reposi-tions himself between them, leaning back on his heels. Planting his palms firmly on my upper thighs, he buries his head in my pussy. His hungry mouth sucks and gnaws at my slick folds and then his talented tongue licks my clit the way a little kid might lick the gravy off a plate. He brings new meaning to breakfast in bed.

He moans. "Mmm, baby, you smell so good. You taste even better. I could eat you morning, noon, and night." The tip of his tongue teases my entrance and then it moves back to my clit...flicking and licking, driving me crazy, while two fingers slide up and down my wet chasm.

I've always had über sensitive nipples, but the nipple clamps seem to be intensifying the sensations I'm feeling down below exponentially. And the more I heave my chest, the tighter they get and the closer I get to the point of no return. A mix of sighs, groans, and whimpers fill the back of my throat and escape through my lips. The clamps give new meaning to the lyrics of that John Mellencamp song, "It Hurts So Good." Oh God, does it! I'm reduced to whimpers and begging to let me come.

Brandon owns all of me. And that includes my orgasms. When they come; where they come; how they come. And that's the way I love him. I can't come until he says I can. Or I'll face the sometimes painful (in a good way!) consequences of disobeying him. I bite down hard on my lip, thinking this will prolong the onset of my orgasm and quell my hunger for him. Wishful thinking! The pain I give myself only adds to the erotic cocktail that's spilling from my core and saturating every cell of my body.

"Please baby, either let me come or fuck me!" Mama taught me that patience had its virtues. But she'd never taught me that patience had its rewards. That's something I've learned from Brandon.

I'm not sure if he's heard my plea. He doesn't respond. His ravenous mouth is too busy devouring me, and the truth is I'm so close to coming he'd deprive me if he stopped. All I can do is cry, "Please, please, please." As far as Brandon's concerned, there's nothing like begging. He loves Mama's magic word. I just have to wait for permission.

My clit is vibrating against his tongue, and inside my belly, the pressure is building, an orgasmic time bomb that will go off when he flicks the switch. And then just when I think I may explode prematurely, he kisses my clit and an orgasm crashes through me. I detonate, shrapnel of bliss spraying me from head to toe as I cry out his name. Oh my God, Oh my God, Oh my God. I'm falling apart cell by cell. He's given me an orgasm of epic proportions. An orgasm I will never forget.

He smacks a hot kiss on my lips. "Happy anniversary, baby."

Happy, happy anniversary.

Brandon

She may not be beautiful by Hollywood standards, but to me she's the most beautiful woman in the world. I love her every imperfection, her luscious curves, her little unexpected dimples. And in the bedroom, she gives me what I need. Many women in the world are in love with me, but not one understands me. Or loves— and reveres—me as much as my Zoey does. Our love has no boundaries. She's insatiable.

She deepens my kiss, cradling my face between her long-fingered hands. The hands that have blown me to pieces innumerable times. Her mouth gnaws mine as our tongues entwine like two dancers, swirling and twirling. She tastes so delicious. And those little gurgling sounds at the base of her throat are such a turn-on. I'm so hard I may burst through my pajama bottom. My hand reaches down to her pussy.

"Brandon," she moans, "you're killing me."

Breathing heavily, I kiss her neck and shoulders, nipping her from time to time. "No, baby, you're going to be the death of me." As I continue to massage her drenched pussy, I place one of her hands on my hard as nails cock. She strokes the length of it.

"Fuck," I mumble under my breath.

"Brandon, fuck me. Please!" she breathes against my neck between succulent wet kisses that are driving me insane. I so fucking love when she begs. But she's going to have to wait. I call the shots here.

"No, baby, not yet," I say, teasing her hot swollen clit and sliding her other hand under the waistband of my bottoms.

"Oh, God, Brandon! I can't take it! I need you in-side me. Please! Pretty please!"

Oh, she's desperate alright. But so am I. "No, baby, not until you've eaten *your* breakfast. And swallowed every drop of it."

Her knowing eyes narrow seductively at me. "Oh, so you want me to give you a blowjob, Mr. Taylor? Is that what it'll take?" She licks her lips and my cock stirs.

Plain and simple. "Do it."

On my next breath, my bottoms are pulled down to my knees and her mouth is clamped around my wide crown. I arch back and hiss. Gripping the base, she lowers her mouth on my thick shaft, her tongue trailing along the backside, and takes me all the way. At the same slow speed and intensity, she comes back up.

"Jesus, Zoey." Seriously, I don't know how she does it. I can't tell you how many times I fantasized her giving me a blowjob before we were married, but nothing prepared me for the earth-shattering reality. An artist, she swirls her tongue around my crown and then goes down on me again, but this time faster with a little scrape of her teeth. She quickly gets into a rhythm and begins pumping the base with her hand. And humming her favorite song—"Unforgettable."

Arching, I squeeze my eyes shut and fist her hair as she bops up and down my monstrous erection because I just need something to hold on to. My breathing is harsh. I can't even get words out of my mouth. Just a bunch of grunts and groans. My fingers continue to strum her throbbing clit. Usually, I can hang on, but my stamina is waning as she sucks me fast and furiously. My body's heating, my pulse racing. Every muscle in my body tenses with ecstasy. I feel my balls contract as my cock prepares for an out of this world orgasm.

"Zo, I'm going to come in your mouth."

She nods with acknowledgment as she goes down on me, the rhythm of her bobbing head bringing me to the brink. As the tip of my cock hits the base of her throat, I explode and cry out her name. Stars and fireworks fill my head. If there's such a thing as a full-body orgasm, I've had one. I think I've gone to heaven.

Her lips stay glued to my cock as I empty my load. God, I love it when she swallows. Then, slowly, I glide my still hard cock out of her mouth, relishing the feeling of her warm velvety tongue following my ascent. She reverently kisses my shimmering crown when I pull out, sucking off the last bit of cum. Four little words: The. Best. Blowjob. Ever.

I suck in a calming breath. "Fuck, baby. That was amazing!"

She smiles with smug victory and then licks her wet pouty lips. The small gesture is so erotic my cock jumps to full attention. I so badly want to be inside her.

"Okay, baby, you're ready for a good fucking. Spread your legs."

She smolders her eyes. "Not yet."

What the fuck? I give the orders in the bedroom.

Before I can get my mouth to move, she leaps out of the bed.

"I'll be right back." She skips out of the room, leaving me pissed as hell. I'm going to have to punish her.

Leaning back against the mountain of pillows, I stare down at my enormous erection as I contemplate Plan B. I didn't want to punish her on our special day, but she's given me no choice. She's got to learn a lesson about who's in control. My mind races. Hmm…handcuffs. I'll use the pair her father gave me and cuff her to the railings of our steel headboard while she's facing it on her knees. First, she's going to get a nice spanking until her sweet ass turns a lovely rosy red. Then, I'm going to taunt that tight pussy of hers. Tease that sweet little clit until she pleads for me to make her come. Except I'm not going to let her. She's going to have to wait just the way she made me wait. And then I'm finally going to use that little toy she bought me. Ha ha! The Magic Cock Ring. The package promises I can go forever before climaxing. I can picture the scene in my mind's eye. Oh yeah. My feisty little wife is going to pay the price. I'm going to fuck her in the ass—that gorgeous puckered hole of hers that's made for me. Bang her like there's no tomorrow and she's going to be begging so hard for me to either stop or make her come she'll be in tears. My cock is twitching at the thought. I mentally high five myself.

"Darling, I'm back," comes a sexy rasp that startles

me out of my wicked reverie. Zoey.

I look up and my eyes stay riveted on her delicious-ly curvy body as she lopes my way. Gucci follows her, wagging his tail. She's holding a small rectangular box in her hand. It's wrapped in metallic paper and finished off with a violet ribbon that's tied in a bow.

Crawling back onto the bed, she sits cross-legged, angled so she's facing me and a breath away. She holds the gift-wrapped box in her palms. My plans for world domination are waylaid by my curiosity.

"What's that?"

After smacking a chaste kiss on my cheek, she hands me the box. "It's *your* anniversary present."

A brow lifts. "Another sex toy?" I ask, untying the ribbon.

"Kind of."

Tearing off the shiny paper, I study the two by six inch generic white box. "Some kind of magic wand?"

"Yes." She smiles coyly. "I hope you love it as much as I do."

I'm getting excited. This could be fun. I feel her gaze on me as I lift off the lid. My eyes almost pop out of their sockets. Holy shit! I know what this is. My character, Kurt Kussler, was given the exact same magic stick by his wife Alisha just before her tragic death. I feel my eyes water.

"Really?" I choke out the word while The Gooch gives a woof.

My beautiful Zoey cups my face with her hands and then tenderly kisses my lips. "Yes, my darling hero. We're having a baby."

Overwhelmed with emotion, I take her in my arms and hold her against my heart, never wanting to let her go. The playroom we were planning to build for ourselves to indulge our lifestyle may be sacrificed for another with a different set of swings.

Brandon

Five Years Later

"Man, did you ever think you'd be thirty-five-years-old sitting on the ledge of a sandbox?"

I'm at the celebrity-filled Beverly Glen Park I frequent regularly. My best bud, Blake Burns, adjusts his shades as we watch our kids play with pails and shovels. He chuckles. "Fuck no."

"Me neither. It's a good life though, huh?"

"I wouldn't trade it in for the world."

"Where's Jen?" I ask him, after checking on The Gooch, who's taking a nap under a nearby tree.

"She's with the new baby at a *Combat Wombats* voice recording session." His talented wife now runs Conquest Broadcasting's popular children's network,

Peanuts.

"Bella and Teddy both love that show."

Bella Angel and Teddy Paul are our twins, my beautiful daughter named after my late mentor, who peacefully passed away just before their birth, and Zoey's mother, and my adorable Teddy, after my father Edward and Zoey's dad Paul. Twins run in Zoey's family, and a generation didn't pass us by. Her parents, Pete and Jo, are the most doting and wonderful grandparents anyone could ask for.

Blake smiles. "Leo loves it too. But his favorite is your show. He goes around the house saying, "Get it! Got it? Good!"

I laugh. In my wildest imagination, I never thought *Kurt Kussler* would be spun off into a super-successful, pro-social animated series. *Kurt Kussler: Bully Buster*. In addition to voicing the main character, I do the live-action wraparounds, condemning bullies and giving tools to kids for dealing with them. It was Blake's wife's idea. Not only is the show a big hit, *Kurt Kussler* action toys are flying off the shelves.

While the animated *Kurt Kussler* will likely be on for years to come, my live action show wrapped up its final season. In the very last episode, Kurt finally destroys his nemesis, The Locust, in an action-packed chase scene that culminates with him going over a cliff, and his wife, Mel, gives birth to twins after years of infertility. I'm sad to see the series end, but I'm moving on to bigger things. I'm going to be the next James

Bond! A part I agreed to only if Zoey was cast as Miss Moneypenny. The producers acquiesced and we start filming this summer. We're both super excited.

A sweet little voice grabs my attention. Teddy. "Daddy, look at my castle!"

My eyes shift to my little boy, who's a spitting image of me—violet eyes and all. His castle is just a pile of sand, but I give him a thumbs-up. My angelic Bella, with her mane of flaming red hair, faces me and yells she helped. I blow her a kiss, and with a big smile, she blows one back with her little hands. God, my little ones are cute. Too cute. I'm so blessed. Too blessed. Zo and I are working on having more kids. Could I possibly have another as delicious as these two munchkins?

Blake cuts into my thoughts. "What's Zoey up to?"

"She's shooting a scene of *Perfect 10* at Musso's today. It's the only day the restaurant is closed and available."

"That show is killing it in the ratings. There's a lot of talk that she's going to be nominated for both a Golden Globe and an Emmy."

"No kidding?" An ear-to-ear grin stretches across my face. Wouldn't that be something if we *both* won this year!?

"Hi, boys!" A familiar flamboyant voice sounds in my ears

My eyes flit to the right. Heading our way is Zoey's brother Jeffrey and his spouse Chaz. They're pushing a stroller. Seated inside it are their adorable two-year-old twin daughters. Elsa and Anna.

Chaz unstraps them. "Okay, beautiful princesses, go play." Clutching their sand toys, they toddle into the sandbox. Looks like our little sandcastle builders are about to get some company. The children spot each other and run up to one and other. Hugs all around. It's so damn cute I take a picture with my cell phone and send it to Zo.

Jeffrey and Chaz squat down next to us. They're wearing matching lime green shorts and floral-print shirts. According to Blake's wife Jennifer, the fashionistas are going through a Lilly Pulitzer whoever-the-fuck-that-is phase. Even their twins are clad in bright floral rompers.

"Did you hear the news?" coos Jeffrey, never one to hold back gossip. "Katrina Moore is being released from prison this week."

"FUCK!" Blake and I shout out in unison. A nearby mom shoots us a dirty look.

Every muscle in my body clenches. The fucking psycho bitch almost robbed Blake of his life and his beautiful wife while she almost robbed me of my life, my bank account, and my career. Blake actually thinks she went after me to bring him and Conquest Broadcasting down. Rob the network of its number one star and everything can change. Who knows? He may be right. The psycho bitch is capable of anything.

Before I can say another word, a nanny comes up to

me and asks for my autograph. With a forced smile, I sign the *Kurt Kussler* novel she's brought along. Jeffrey and Chaz excuse themselves and saunter over to the ice cream truck to buy treats for all the kids. I ask Blake how he feels about Katrina's release.

"You know what, I'm not going to worry about it. Jen and I have some dirt on her that will keep her from trying anything rash. And you know what, pal…if I were you, I'd just forget about her."

I digest his words and think about his father's words of wisdom he once shared: "Some things are best forgotten." I come to the conclusion he's right. Thanks to Zoey, the incriminating photos Katrina took with her phone in Cannes have long been deleted and there's nothing she can do or say to hurt me. I'm going to bury that regrettable bitch in that part of mind where memories don't exist. Make her forgettable.

There's only one woman who matters in my life. My wonderful, sexy as hell wife, and tonight I'm going give her a fucking that'll be unforgettable.

Katrina

California Institution for Women, Chino

My last fucking supper. Goodbye, suckers. I'm out of this hellhole tomorrow. It's been five long years of pure torture. Whoever said "orange is the new black" needs their stupid head examined. In less than twenty-four hours, I'll be out of these rags and back in Armani. And drinking Cristal.

After I toast my new life, I know exactly what I'm doing next. I glare down at my chest. Skeletons of the letters are still there; those bullshit laser treatments were a painful waste of time. I should have asked for my money back. But I've decided, why try to cover them up? I'm going to get them re-inked. Except I'm going to replace the "u" with an "i" and dot it with a crown. B-I-T-C-H. Because I'm still the Queen of Bitches.

I've learned a lot. Men…they're all fucking assholes. Blake, Brandon, Scott, even Daddy. Mommy had the right idea when she chose Monique.

The world needs to know. Yes, I'm going to write a book. In fact, I've been working on it in prison. Such a great title: *I Put the It in Bitch*.

It's going to bring me fame and fortune. Everything I've always wanted.

Fuck them all.

FADE TO BLACK

Note from Nelle

Dearest Reader~

Thank you for sharing Brandon and Zoey's story. If you loved it, I hope you will consider leaving a review. Even a very short one helps others discover my books and means the world to me. You can find links to the books at various retailers on my website.

Nelle Website:

nellelamour.com/unforgettable-series

I now want to share something personal with you. As you all know, *Unforgettable* was inspired by the beautiful song of that name sung by the late great Nat King Cole and his daughter, Natalie. Natalie sadly passed away while I was finishing the edit of *Unforgettable 3*. I was greatly saddened by the untimely passing of this amazing talent. What's more, she left us on New Year's Eve, the very day my unforgettable father died several years ago. *Unforgettable 1* was dedicated to my father. I find this so uncanny. Fate has her own way of making things happen.

If you haven't read my bestselling *THAT MAN* series—the epic story of Blake Burns and his tiger, Jennifer McCoy—I highly recommend you do. You will laugh, cry, and swoon…and find out what really went down between Blake and evil Katrina. Many readers have asked if they will see more of the *THAT MAN* characters as well as those from *Unforgettable,* including Katrina. The answer is yes. My upcoming standalone romantic comedy tentatively entitled *Spermed* features characters from both in cameos. I've also started a story about Jen's best friend, Libby, and I'm toying with the idea of a Katrina story as well as a Christmas reunion novella that will bring all the characters together. Email me at nellelamour@ gmail.com and let me know your thoughts. I'm especially interested to know: Do you think Katrina could ever reform and go from her evil self to someone with a heart?

There's no rest for the weary. I'm off to start writing again and I can't wait to bring you more books. I feel very blessed to have such a passionate fan base. Every comment and message on Facebook brings a big smile to my face, and both your reviews and emails have brought me many happy tears. Don't stop them from coming as I love hearing from you. You, my Nelle's Belles, are the reason I write.

Be sure sign up for my newsletter and follow me both Amazon BookBub to hear about ARC giveaways, new releases, and sales.

Newsletter Sign Up:

http://eepurl.com/N3AXb

Amazon Author Page:

amazon.com/Nelle-LAmour/e/B00ATHR0LQ

BookBub:

bookbub.com/settings/authors#authors-search

MWAH!~Nelle ♥

Acknowledgments

I used to say it takes a village to write a book. But you know what…it takes a world—readers. My readers hail from continent to continent, country to country. From the biggest cities to farmlands. I'm so in awe. So, I'm thanking all of you first. Without you, I couldn't be a writer. A special thanks goes to those who have written a review, emailed me, PM'd me on Facebook and have commented or shared one of my posts. I can't begin to tell you how much that means to me.

Next, I want to acknowledge my incredible Beta team. Each and every one of them contributes something special to my books. They're smart, they're honest, and they make me laugh too! They're as much my first readers as they are my dear friends. So, in alphabetical order, here is the incredible Beta Team for *Unforgettable 3:* Gemma Cocker, Kellie Fox, Kashunnah Fly, Jennifer Martinez, Shannon Meadows Hayward, Gloria Herrera, Jenn Moshe, Kim Pinard-Newsome, Sheena Reid, Karen Silverstein, Jeanette Sinfield, Mary Jo Toth, and Joanna Warren. I love you and thank you all!

I need to single out a few. First, Gloria Hererra, who's gone on to become my trusted and beloved PA. I don't know what I'd do without her. Writing and promoting, I've learned, are two full-time jobs, and Gloria has taken it upon herself to handle most of the latter necessary evil, allowing me the opportunity to devote myself mostly to writing. She's amazing, and I hope you agree her Facebook teasers and videos are outstanding. Best of all, she makes me roar with laughter with her wicked sense of humor and dirty mind when I want to pull out my hair!

Next, Mary Jo Toth, who has become my spot-on proofreader. I don't know how she does it, but she sees things I never see—even after I've read over what I've written a gazillion times. And she's so good at helping me with sayings and idioms, which I can never get right. I'm a grammatic fanatic, but am also the one who once wrote: "Kill two stones with one bird." I kid you not!

Last, the incredible Jeanette Sinfield. Finishing *Unforgettable 3* was super hard for me because I was on the verge of burning out. However, Jeanette allowed me to send her each chapter, revision by revision. Honestly, her input and support got me through. She was my muse and cheerleader and I am eternally grateful. I adore you! And will never forget your love and support.

Another big shout out goes to my amazing team of

ARC readers, too many to list, who read and reviewed all three parts of *Unforgettable.* Your heartfelt words made me both laugh and cry. I wish you could have heard me every time the word AWWWW!! spilled from my lips. Thank you! Thank you!

Talking about reviews, hats off to all the bloggers who read and reviewed *Unforgettable* and spread the word. Special mention goes to Mollien Osterman/Alpha Book Club, Jennifer Pierson/The Power of Three Readers, Nikki Costello/Crazy Cajun Book Addicts, Lorena Garcia/Brittany's Book Blog, Stephanie Johnson/Crazy for Books, Ellen Widom/The Book Bellas, and Johnnie-Marie Howard. And a big shout out to Give Me Books Promotions, who tirelessly spearheaded by Cover Releases and Release Blitzes. I adore you, Kylie McDermott and George Turney.

Writing a novel, let alone a trilogy, can be a very lonely, frustrating, and daunting process, and there were many times I doubted I would ever hit the "publish" button. Somehow, it never gets easier. A big hug goes to my two BWFs (Best Writer Friends), Arianne Richmonde and Adriane Leigh, who kept me sane. What would I do without your emails, your love, and your support? And all the laughs too! I also want to thank authors, CD Reiss, Alessandra Torre, Lauren Blakely, Whitney Gracia Williams, Vanessa Booke, Avery Aster, and Fifi Flowers for their willingness to get the word out about my series. By the way, if you haven't read books by these amazing authors, you should! They're fantastic!

Now, we're down to the end. My gratitude to Paul Salvette/BB eBooks, my brilliant formatter, who accommodated all my revisions so graciously, and my awesome cover artist, Arijana Karcic/Cover it! Designs, who designed all my fabulous covers. You're stuck with me for life!

Finally, my family. Please don't hate me! I know I've been the worst mommy ever, but this is my life. And with college around the corner, my girls, this is what I must do. I made a New Year's resolution to create more balance in my life, but don't count on it. It's just not the way I roll. I love you all the more for putting up with me.

Okay, last but not least, my hubby. Thank you for taking on so many of the mommy responsibilities and for keeping me supplied with an endless amount of Trident gum, popcorn, and Diet Coke. And for still loving me, no matter how whacked out I get. You will always be unforgettable.

Nelle L'Amour is a *New York Times* and *USA Today* bestselling author who lives in Los Angeles with her Prince Charming-ish husband, twin teenage princesses, and a bevy of royal pain-in-the-butt pets. A former executive in the entertainment industry with a prestigious Humanitas Prize for promoting human dignity and freedom to her credit, she gave up playing with Barbies a long time ago, but still enjoys playing with toys with her husband. While she writes in her PJs, she loves to get dressed up and pretend she's Hollywood royalty. Her steamy stories feature characters that will make you laugh, cry, and swoon and stay in your heart forever.

To learn about her new releases, sales, and giveaways, please sign up for her newsletter and follow her on social media. Nelle loves to hear from her readers.

Check out her cool website:
www.nellelamour.com

Sign up for her fun newsletter:
http://eepurl.com/N3AXb

Join her on Facebook:
facebook.com/NelleLamourAuthor

Follow her on Twitter:
twitter.com/nellelamour

Email her at:
nellelamour@gmail.com

Follow Her on Amazon:
amazon.com/Nelle-LAmour/e/B00ATHR0LQ

89017509R00155

Made in the USA
Columbia, SC
16 February 2018